ROAD TRIPPIN' WITH MY WITCHES

A WITCH SQUAD COZY MYSTERY

M.Z. ANDREWS

Road Trippin' with My Witches
A Witch Squad Cozy Mystery: Book #9

by
M.Z. Andrews

Copyright © M.Z. Andrews 2018

ISBN: 9781729471982
ASIN: B07K1S1DQC
VS: 10072019.03

Cover Art by: Arrigo Verderosa
Contact email: verderosa.arrigo@gmail.com
Editing by: Clio's Editing

This book is dedicated to Kris, my old road tripping buddy.
May your car always drive in the right direction.
May the roads always be clear of barbed wire.
May the ditches be shallow.
May you always find enough change between the seats to share a cheeseburger with a friend.
And may the cops never be able to keep up with you.
Love you,
M

CHAPTER 1

I ground the remnants of a midafternoon nap out of my eyes and peered up at my overly zealous sprite of a roommate. "Seriously, Jax?" I groaned. "I was trying to take a nap."

Jumping onto my bed on her knees, she bounced up and down animatedly. "You've been sleeping forever, Mercy. It's time to start packing! Come on, get up!" she begged, her high-pitched voice squeakier than usual. "Get up, get up, get up." She chanted the words in rhythm with her bouncing.

I groaned, rolled onto my back, and hooked my elbow over my eyes to block the light she'd just turned on. "Omigosh, Jax. Can you *be* any more annoying?"

"Probably," she said with a giggle. "Now, come on. It's time to pack."

"Pack? Jax, we're not leaving until tomorrow, and we're only gonna be gone for three days. It's gonna take me like five minutes to throw a couple pairs of shorts and tank tops into a duffle bag."

Sniffling, Jax swiped a hand across the bottom of her

nose and then stared at me like I'd just cussed her out. "Mercy!" she breathed. "You have to bring extra clothes. You know, just in case."

"Just in case of what?"

"You know. You need your swimming suit in case we stay somewhere that has a pool. You need a nice dress in case we meet some cute boys and get invited to a party. You need sneakers in case we decide we want to go on a hike. You need a sweater in case it's chilly. You know it gets chilly in the mountains even if it is almost summer."

"Jax. Jersey City is literally like a five-hour drive from Aspen Falls. With bathroom breaks, six hours *at the most*. I seriously don't think I need all that stuff. Plus we can't all bring tons of stuff or it's not all going to fit in Sweets' car."

Jax sniffled again. "Reign said he'd help us put whatever doesn't fit in her trunk onto the roof."

I pulled my arm off my face and peered at Jax with one narrowed eye. "Why are you sniffling? Are you getting sick?"

She put her flattened palm against her nose and wiggled it. "No. I think it's just allergies." She sniffled again like she was trying to hold back a sneeze.

"You better not be getting sick. I don't want to ride around in a car with you for three days and have you get me sick. I hate being sick."

"I'm not going to get you sick, Mercy."

I hooked my arm back over my face again. "You better not."

Just then our door flew open and Holly came breezing into our bedroom. "Guys! It's here! My package is finally here!" She tossed a large cardboard box onto the bed.

I heard the bathroom door down the hallway open, and seconds later, Alba appeared in our room behind Holly with a spell book tucked beneath her arm. "The mail came? Was there anything in there for me?" Hope filled her voice.

"It wasn't the mailman," said Holly as she grabbed a pair of scissors off Jax's desk and sliced the packing tape off the large box. "It was the UPS man."

Alba's shoulders folded inward and her face crumpled. "Oh."

Resigning myself to the fact that nap time was now officially over, I forced myself into a sitting position. "What's in the package?"

Holly rubbed her hands together and let out a little squeal. "My new summer wardrobe. Just in time for our trip."

Jax looked over at me triumphantly as if Holly ordering a new wardrobe had somehow justified her wanting me to start packing.

I rolled my eyes. "You had to get an entire new wardrobe for a three-day road trip?"

Alba curled her lip. "Sounds excessive if you ask me."

"Well, I wasn't asking you, now was I?" snapped Holly before plowing into her box, pulling out blouse after blouse, a few dresses, several skirts, a couple pairs of shorts, and even a few pairs of coordinating sandals. She held up a strappy pair of gold wedge sandals. "Oooh, girls! Look at these! Aren't they fabulous?"

I stared at the mountain of clothing she'd unpacked. "Geez, Holly. How can you afford all that?"

She blinked her crystalline-blue eyes back at me like she didn't understand the question. "It's a care package from Daddy."

"Must be rough," said Alba gruffly.

"Your dad seriously picked out all those clothes for you?" asked Jax, her own blue eyes wide.

Holly waved a hand dismissively. "Oh, I doubt it. His new girlfriend probably picked everything out. Daddy said she did costume design on his last film. I think she's, like, into fashion or something."

"I'm so jealous," whispered Jax.

"I know, right?" Holly giggled. Then, right in front of us, she pulled off the soft V-neck she wore and wiggled out of her white cut-off shorts.

"Seriously, Cosmo? You can't even do that behind a closed door?" barked Alba, rushing to shut the door.

Holly watched her curiously. "What's the big deal? My mom and I used to walk around our house in our underwear all the time. We're all girls here."

"Yeah, except my brother's just downstairs," I said.

"Oh, I didn't think of Reign," she said, a wicked smile on her face.

I rolled my eyes. "Sure you didn't."

Holly put a hand on her hip. "Besides, women should be proud of their bodies. I know I'm proud of mine."

"We've noticed," said Alba.

Standing in only her panties and little more than a Band-Aid for a bra, Holly pulled on one of her new dresses. It was formfitting and clung to her shapely assets. She spun around several times, watching the short skirt flare at her hips. "This is so adorable!"

"It's really cute," Jax agreed. "You gonna let me borrow it sometime?"

Holly lifted a shoulder. "Sure! If it fits, of course."

I snorted air out my nose. We all knew it wouldn't fit. Even though Holly wasn't much taller than Jax, she filled out every piece of clothing she owned, while clothes typically hung off Jax's super slender frame.

But Jax seemed satisfied with that answer. She shot Holly a megawatt smile. "Yay!"

Alba hitched her thumb over her shoulder. "Listen, I'm gonna go downstairs and see if the mail came yet."

"You expecting something?" I asked her.

"Yeah. Hey, why don't you guys bring the map downstairs, and we'll plan out our route for the trip tomorrow? Sweets is supposed to be off work any minute, so we can go over it together."

Holding up a flattened palm, Holly quirked a brow. "Easy, there, Indiana Jones. We're not looking for the lost ark. I'll just Google the directions on my phone. Easy peasy."

Alba rolled her eyes. "Yeah, well, alright, genius, and what happens if we're going through the mountains and we lose our signal?"

"I don't know. Then we'll follow the sun."

"And if it's dark?"

"Geez, Alba, relax! Then we'll pull over and get directions."

"Yeah, well, if we had a map in the car, then we'd always know exactly where we were, wouldn't we?"

Jax cocked her head sideways. "You sure they even make maps anymore, Alba?"

"Of course I'm sure they still make maps. Red was supposed to pick one up the other day at the gas station." She glanced over at me. "You managed to handle that between naps, right?"

"Your humor astounds me, Alba," I snapped. "Yes, as a matter of fact, I handled it."

"Good." She shook her head as if she were tired of talking to us. "I'm going downstairs. Just meet me down there, and bring the map. We have work to do."

After Alba disappeared into the hallway, Jax pointed at an envelope at the bottom of Holly's box. She plucked it out and held it up. "What's this, Holly?"

"Ooh, a letter from Daddy!" said Holly, her eyes lighting up. She tore open the envelope and unfolded the paper. A small black card dropped onto the floor. Ignoring it, she read the letter aloud. "My dearest Holly, I'm so proud of you for completing your first year of college. I'm sorry you weren't able to make it home with the ticket I bought for you. Just let me know when you're ready to come home and I'll send you a new one. Since you weren't able to do spring break, I think a road trip with your girlfriends is an excellent idea. In addition to the new wardrobe that Abby picked out for you, I'm enclosing a credit card, which should take care of all necessary expenses for you and your friends on your trip. Enjoy! You've earned it! Love, Dad." Holly squealed excitedly as she picked the black card up from the floor. "Girls! He gave me his *black card*!"

"What's a black card?" asked Jax.

"What's a black card?!" breathed Holly, astounded by such a question. "Only the most *elite* of all credit cards! Wow! I can't believe he actually gave me his black card. He's never even let me touch it before!"

I shook my head. "I can't believe he just gives you whatever you want, Holly. I didn't realize how spoiled you were."

"Spoiled? I'm not spoiled."

I surged forward and snapped the black card out of Holly's hands. "Your father just gave you and all of your friends an all-expenses-paid road trip and an entirely new wardrobe. That's not spoiled?"

"I wouldn't say I'm spoiled. Maybe I'm *lucky*."

"Holly, Mercy's right," said Jax with a shrug. "You're

spoiled. But I don't see anything wrong with it. I wish my dad were around to spoil me."

I frowned. "I don't. My dad never wanted to be in my life so good riddance. I don't know why you'd want your dad around either, Jax. You're in the same boat as me."

Jax shrugged. "I'm a lot more forgiving than you are, Mercy."

Holly smiled. "She's got you there, Merc!" She bounced on her toes and headed for the door. "Okay, enough depressing chitchat. I'm gonna go downstairs and see what Reign thinks about my new dress."

When she'd gone, Jax looked over at me. "Come on, Mercy, let's go downstairs and plan our route. You've got the map, right?"

I pointed across the room. "Yeah. Over there. But Sweets isn't even here yet. Maybe I'll just nap until she gets here." I yawned and slumped sideways onto the pillow beside me. It'd been a busy year, and I still didn't feel like I'd caught up on my sleep.

Suddenly our door burst open again. "Hey, girls!" said Sweets, dropping her purse on the bed. "Alba said we're going to go over our route for tomorrow. Mercy, do you have the map?"

I groaned. My nap would have to wait for another day. "Ugh. Yeah. Let's go."

CHAPTER 2

With both a Pennsylvania map and a New Jersey map spread across one of the dining room tables, the five of us pored over our route while devouring Habernackle's dinner special: fried chicken, corn, mashed potatoes and country gravy. It was comfort food at its finest.

"Mmm," said Sweets, licking the grease from her fingers. "This is *sooo yummy*."

"Yeah," agreed Jax with a drumstick to her lips. "It's amazing."

Alba wiped her fingers on a napkin and then pointed at the map. "I think we're just gonna go down to the turnpike and take that all the way to Harrisburg. Then we'll take I-81 and then eventually I-78. It looks like the fastest route."

Sweets stopped licking her fingers to look up at Alba sharply. "Get off on I-81? Why can't we just stay on the turnpike?"

"Because that takes us south, and we wanna go north, hello?"

"Yeah, but I wanna go through Philadelphia!"

Alba looked appalled. "Through Philadelphia?! Why? That's totally out of the way."

"Yeah, but I was looking online and there's a Magic Garden in Philadelphia. And a giant glowing paintbrush! And the tallest tombstone in the—"

Cutting in, Alba put a hand up and shook her head. "Are you kiddin' me? No, no, no. We don't need to see a giant glowing paintbrush or the tallest anything. That's ridiculous." Shaking her head resolutely, she pointed at the map. "No. We do what I said and take I-76 to I-81. It turns into I-78 and takes us right into the city. If no one drinks anything past, say, noon tomorrow, then we won't have to stop and use the restroom. We'll leave the minute Sweets gets off work, and we'll be at my house by eleven at the latest."

Jax, Sweets, and Holly all stared at Alba, horrified.

"B-but it's supposed to be a *road* trip," said Jax with a long face. "I thought we were gonna do some *fun* stuff. You know, eat lots of snacks and stop at cool places and sing road trip karaoke. I made a mixtape."

Sweets nodded. "Yeah. I thought that was the point of all of us driving together. Alba, you said the wedding isn't until Monday anyway. Why do we have to be there on Friday night? What'll we do all weekend?"

Holly wrinkled her nose. "And while you're at it, can you explain to me why anyone would want to get married on a *Monday*?"

"Not that it's any of your business, but if you must know, my brother's getting married on a Monday because it's cheaper than getting married on a weekend. And they picked Memorial Day because it made more sense to close the business on a holiday than a regular day. That way no one has to take any time off work, and it's not gonna cost anyone much money."

Holly lifted her brows and swung her eyes down towards the table. "Sounds like a *fabulous* wedding," she muttered under her breath.

Wiping my mouth, I glanced across the table at Alba. "Yeah, you know, Alba, the girls have a point. This road trip isn't just about driving you home for the summer. It's supposed to be kind of our last hurrah until the fall. I figured we'd at least stop at a couple of cool roadside attractions along the way."

"Sweets, what time are you getting off work tomorrow?" asked Alba.

Sweets shrugged. "It depends on how long it takes me to clean the place up. The absolute earliest would be five thirty, but it might not be until six."

"Let's just say we don't leave until six. What exactly do you think is gonna be open after six o'clock on a Friday night along the interstate?"

It was obvious I was going to have to talk some sense into Alba. "Fine, then we don't take the interstate. We drive partway tomorrow night. We crash at some cheap motel, and then we finish the trip Saturday. Even if we dinked around all day in Philly on Saturday, that *still* gets you home in plenty of time for the wedding. And we have time to turn around and get Sweets back in time to get to work on Tuesday."

Alba let her head roll back on her shoulders. "Five broads in a cheap motel on the interstate? Yeah, Red. That sounds like an incredible idea." She shook her head. "Incredibly *stupid*."

"First of all, we're *witches*, Alba. We can defend ourselves, right?"

Alba wouldn't make eye contact and instead just shrugged.

"And second of all, we don't have to stay on the interstate. We could stay somewhere in Philly. If Sweets wants to stop at a few touristy places there, then we find a decent place to stay and we head out in the morning."

"Ugh," groaned Alba. "You guys are making this harder than it needs to be."

"So are you, Alba," said Holly. "This is supposed to be a fun trip."

"Yeah, well, I really don't have the funds to make this a fun trip. Tony was supposed to send me some money, but it's still not here. If it's not here by tomorrow, I'll barely be able to afford to chip in for gas. And even staying at a cheap motel ain't free, ya know."

"Oh!" said Holly brightly as Reign approached the table. "You didn't hear me tell the girls. Daddy said he'd pay for the whole trip. Gas money, hotel money, food, everything. He gave me his black card!" She pulled the card out of her bra and flashed it at Alba.

"That was really nice of your dad, Holly, but we'll still pitch in," said Sweets. "I've hardly spent any of my paychecks for the last few months. I can afford to help out."

Alba shook her head as she looked at Holly. "It doesn't bother you, just taking your pop's money like that?"

Holly lifted her shoulder and frowned. "No? He's my dad. Why would it bother me?"

"Oh, I don't know. Maybe because you're an *adult*. Because it's about time you learned to stand on your own two feet? First he sent you a whole box of new clothes. Now he's paying for you to run around and play games for the summer. Are you gonna let him do that forever?"

The way Holly pulled her head back and lifted her

brows told us all that she'd really never given that any thought. "He wants to do it," she said, glancing up at Reign uncomfortably. "I mean, it's not like I have a job. I'm in school right now."

"That's the thing, though. You're *not* in school right now," said Alba. "You should be getting a summer job like the rest of us. Shorty and Red are helpin' Linda out by waitin' tables here at the B&B. Sweets busts her butt day in and day out at the bakery. I'll be put to work the second my feet touch the state line, but you, you're just livin' the high life off Daddy's dime? What happens when you get married someday? You just expect some poor schmuck to foot the bill for you?"

Holly swallowed hard. Her eyes were glossy as she glanced up at my brother. "What do *you* think, Reign? Is it bad that my dad still pays for everything?"

My brother lifted a shoulder uncomfortably. I could tell that he didn't like being put on the spot like that. "I mean, it's really none of my business. I never had anyone around to pay my way, so I wouldn't know."

Alba gestured towards him. "See? Even Slick here knows the meaning of an honest day's work."

"But he's my dad," said Holly, a little less assuredly this time. "Dads are supposed to take care of their little girls. Sweets, doesn't your dad pay for things for you?"

"Mmm. Not really. I mean, as far as clothes, I mostly got hand-me-downs from my sisters or my cousins, and I babysat in high school to pay for my car and for gas money. I had to take out student loans for witch school. There were too many kids in my family for Dad to afford to pay for all of us to go to college."

Holly frowned. "Oh."

Sweets looked at Holly sadly. "Oh! He did send me fifty

dollars last semester when I blew that tire on my car and needed to get a new one. But that was before I was getting paid at the bakery."

"Hey, Sweets, speaking of your car, you took it in for an oil change like I told you to, right?" asked Alba.

Sweets' head dipped. "Yes, I did."

"Did you have them check the fuel filter?"

"Mmm, I'm not sure. I assume they did."

"You didn't ask?"

Sweets took a sip of her drink and then shook her head. "No. Why would I ask?"

"Well, when was the last time you had it changed?"

Sweets looked at Alba blankly and shrugged. "Like I know? My dad took care of that kind of stuff."

Holly's brows lifted as she pointed emphatically at Sweets. "See! It's normal for girls to rely on their dads for stuff."

Alba groaned and shot Holly a scowl. "Hey, at least she *has* a car."

"I have a car! It's just in California."

"Yeah? You buy it with your own money?"

Holly's face fell.

Alba nodded. "I thought so." She turned her attention back on Sweets. "Listen, the other day when I borrowed it to return some books to the Great Witch's Library, it stalled out on me. Maybe you should take it back in before we leave tomorrow."

Sweets cocked her head sideways. "Alba, there's no way the mechanic is going to get it looked at tomorrow. Besides, I said it's fine. I haven't noticed anything, and I drive it every day."

"You drive it like two blocks from here to the bakery."

"Your point?"

Alba pursed her lips. "My point is, if something happens on the ride, I'm blaming you."

Sweets shrugged and bit a piece of chicken off her drumstick. "You go on right ahead, Alba. If something happens to my car, I'll take full responsibility."

CHAPTER 3

"You gotta be kiddin' me!" Alba stared wide-eyed at the pile of luggage covering one of Habernackle's dining room tables. "How can you morons possibly need this much stuff to go on a three-day road trip?!"

Jax's gaze skipped across the table sheepishly and landed on the floor, where two duffle bags, a laundry basket full of odds and ends, and a pile of bedding shoved into a black garbage bag sat stacked on top of each other. "Well, Alba, for starters, that pile's yours."

Alba's arms waved dramatically. "I'm moving home for the summer!" she bellowed. "That's everything I own! What's your excuse?"

Holly, who had just skipped down the stairs, tossed another bag on the pile. "Can you believe I *almost* forgot my makeup bag?" She tossed her head back, making her blond hair sway behind her. "Can you imagine? That would have been horrible!"

"The world as we know it would've ended," snapped Alba dryly. She lifted several of the bags to inspect what all was there and then finally shook her head. "No way. We aren't bringing this much stuff. There's not enough room. Each of you gets to bring one bag."

"One bag!" squealed Jax.

I shrugged and pointed at the backpack I'd shoved some shorts and a few t-shirts in earlier. "I only have one bag. Everything else is Jax's and Holly's. Sweets doesn't even have her stuff down here yet."

"All of this is just Shorty's and Cosmo's?!" She stared at Holly. "You can't be serious. It's *three* days! And we're gonna be in a car most of the time! Whaddaya need all these bags for?"

Holly plumped out her bottom lip. "I like to be prepared in case of emergencies."

"Oh yeah? You got stuff in there to change a tire or extra flashlights or something?"

"Eww. No. I packed all the new clothes Daddy sent me, but then I had to add a few extra outfits for all the possible scenarios."

"Possible scenarios? What're you talkin' about?"

"You know, like I don't know what kind of things we're going to do. What if we go out to a fancy dinner? I'll need a couple of choices for my outfits. Or what if we decide to go out dancing? Or what if we hit up a spa?"

"Dancing? A fancy dinner? The spa? This ain't Club Med, Cosmo! It's literally gonna take us six hours to get from here to Jersey and then it's going to take you six hours to get home. You can pack two changes of clothing and your makeup. That's all we've got room for!"

Holly fingered her bags before looking up at Alba defiantly. "Since when are you the queen of this road trip, Alba? Its Sweets' car, and I'm paying for gas, food, and lodging!"

Alba wagged her finger in the air in front of Holly's face.

"Oh, no, no, *you're* not payin' for *anything*, princess. *Daddy's* payin' for this trip. So don't go gettin' it twisted."

Jax sighed. "Listen, Alba. It's not that big of a deal. Reign said he's gonna help us get this all on the roof of Sweets' car, and I *need* this stuff." Jax pointed at her backpack, which sat on top of her fuzzy gray blanket, and her favorite stuffed unicorn. "This is the stuff I need for *inside* the car. It's got my books, and my tablet, and my music, and the games I'm bringing..."

"Games? You can't be serious! Why in the world do we need games?"

Jax frowned. "Have you *never* been on a road trip, Alba?"

"Not on one where you take *games*." Alba looked at me. "You ever brought a game on a road trip, Red?"

I shrugged. I hadn't been on many road trips in my life. It was always just me, my mom, and Gran and we never really went anywhere. Once we'd gone to see Mount Rushmore in South Dakota, but I was only like seven. I really didn't remember much about that trip, except that I'd gotten carsick and we'd had to pull over at a car wash so Mom could hose off the floor mats. Even then, the car had still stunk like puke for the rest of the trip.

"Yeah, you're asking the wrong person. I mean, yeah, they probably brought too much stuff, but I don't see the harm in a couple of games. Regardless, I think you're missing the point, Alba. This is supposed to be a fun girls' trip. You agreed to it, remember?"

"Yeah, well, no one told me I was gonna have to play games." She threw her arms up in the air and strode towards the stairs. "You know what? I change my mind. I'm not going. I'd rather take my broomstick back to Jersey than to ride with you losers."

19

"If you take a broomstick, then there's no room for all your stuff. Is there?" Jax taunted with a grin. "Come on, Alba. Turn that frown upside down. This is supposed to be a super fun trip. There's no point in starting the trip off grouchy."

"Shorty, are you gonna be Mary Poppins this whole trip? Because if you are, I'm definitely flying solo. You know I can't handle that cheerful crap."

I'd heard just about enough. I held a hand up. "Alba. We haven't even left yet and you're already on everyone's last nerve. Mine included. This trip was supposed to be about friendship and all that, so you're going to have be a little nicer if we're all going to get along." Then I turned and pointed at Jax and Holly. "And you two got carried away with all this stuff. You can each bring *one* personal belonging in the car, and *one* bag for the roof. That's it. Alba and Sweets get the trunk. Got it?"

"One personal belonging?!" cried Jax. "But Mercy, I *have* to have my backpack and my blanket, and you know I don't go anywhere without Emily!"

"Jax! You are eighteen years old! You don't need a stuffed unicorn on a six-hour car ride!"

"But I use her as a pillow. And she'd be brokenhearted if I left her here all alone."

Alba curled her lip. "Did you seriously just say that your *stuffed animal* is going to be brokenhearted if you leave it here alone?"

Jax frowned. "Alba! Emily isn't just a stuffed animal. She's my bestie. Well, except for you girls."

I groaned. I knew I wasn't going to get anywhere on that topic with Jax. "Fine. You can bring those things for the car, but then only *one* bag for the roof. You too, Holly. One thing for the car and one thing for the roof. Sweets is going to be home any minute, and Reign still has to put all this stuff on the roof, so you better get going. Otherwise we won't get on the road until dark!"

Just then, the kitchen doors burst open and my brother strode out, wiping his hands on a dish towel. "Did I hear my name?"

"Oh, hi, Reign," chirped Holly, rushing over to greet him.

"Hey," he said gruffly. I watched as his eyes glanced over at her and then immediately swung away, as if he was unable to look at her. It made me wonder if Holly had worn out her welcome at the B&B and was getting on his nerves or something.

I pointed at the pile of stuff on the table. "We were just taking about having you strap all this stuff to the roof for us."

His eyes widened. "All of this? Didn't you say you're coming back Monday night after the wedding?"

"Oh, we're not taking it all," said Alba. "Cosmo and Shorty have to repack their stuff. They'll have it ready in a few minutes, cuz we're takin' off the second Sweets walks in that door."

As if on cue, the little doorbell chimed as the front door opened and Sweets strode in. "Are we ready to go?"

∾

"THANKS, REIGN," said Holly, batting her fake eyelashes at him. "I really appreciate your help."

Reign tightened the tie-down he'd used to attach our bags to the roof. As instructed, Holly and Jax had each pared down their essentials to one bag apiece, though Holly had found the largest bag she could and pretty much brought the same amount of stuff she'd packed originally. She'd just managed to stuff it all into one big bag instead of several smaller ones. "Yeah, glad to help," he said, tying the loose strap to the tight one so it wouldn't flap around when we drove.

When he was done, Holly hung onto his elbow and smiled up at him. "Are you gonna miss me?"

Reign glanced over at me uncomfortably and cleared his throat. "Yeah, are you kidding? I'll miss all of you."

I almost felt bad for my brother. Holly was relentless. Bypassing her, I stood up on my tippy-toes and threw my arms around my brother's shoulders. "Alright, we're leaving. See you Monday night. It'll be late. Don't wait up."

Reign hugged me back. "I'll be back Monday night late too. Did you forget I'm taking off when you leave?"

"Oh that's right. Where did you say you're going again?" I asked, letting him go. My brother had mentioned something to me earlier in the week about needing a minute to himself, but that was really all he'd said.

"Just up into the mountains. You know, to clear my head. Cell reception will be spotty, but I'll try and check in with Mom when I can."

I felt bad for my brother. Ever since his dad had left town he'd been quieter than usual. I gave him a tight smile. "Alone in the wilderness with no cell signal? That sounds dangerous."

He gave me a look. "Trust me, Sis. I can handle myself. It's you girls that I'm worried about. Don't do anything stupid, like getting yourselves killed. Okay?"

I grinned. "Yeah, we'll do our best."

He pointed at the trunk. "I threw some sandwiches in a cooler and put them in the trunk. In case anyone gets hungry."

Holly tipped her head sideways. "Aww, Reign. You are just the sweetest ever."

"It's no big deal. I know you guys don't have a lot of money for the trip," he said.

"Wow, thanks, bro," I said, shooting him my closed fist for him to pound.

"Bye, Reign. I'm gonna miss you," chirped Jax, throwing her arms around his waist.

"Later, Nugget." He patted her back. "Take lots of pictures to show me when you get back, will you?"

Jax giggled and nodded as she pulled away, hugging Emily to her chest. "Yeah, of course." Then her eyes brightened. She pulled her phone out of the waistband of her tights. "Hey, can you take a picture of us before we leave?"

"Yeah, sure."

Alba rolled her eyes. "Are you serious right now? Are we literally gonna take a picture every five seconds?"

"Yes, we are, Alba. Get used to it," said Holly. "I brought my selfie stick." As we all assembled in front of Sweets' overpacked car, Holly moved Sweets to her other side. "You're on my good side, Sweets. You stand over here."

"Oh, for the love of—"

"Smile." Reign snapped a picture without even warning us.

"Uh!" cried Jax, still fiddling with her hair. "I wasn't ready!"

Reign sighed and held the camera up again. "Okay, one more pic. Witches' road trip on three. One… two…three!"

"Witches' road trip!"

CHAPTER 4

W hen we hit the turnpike just south of Aspen Falls, Jax pushed her unicorn onto my lap and her blanket onto Holly's lap. Then she reached down to rifle through her backpack. Extracting a CD case, she opened it and then lunged between the two front seats.

"Whoa, whoa, whoa. Where you think you're goin', Shorty?"

Jax turned to look at Alba, inadvertently shoving her butt in my face. "I wanna put in my CD."

"Give it here, I'll put it in. You stay back there."

Staring at Jax's rear end, I leaned my head against the car window. "I call shotgun at the next rest stop."

"You can't call shotgun, Red. I already called it."

"You can't call it for the whole trip, Alba."

"I can call it, and I did. There's no way I'm sitting back there with Shorty and Cosmo for the rest of this trip. I'll go nuts."

"Alba, put that in, pleeeease," begged Jax, shaking her CD between the seats so Alba would take it from her.

Alba wrinkled her nose, looking down at it as if it smelled bad. "What's on it?"

"It's a mixtape I made especially for the trip."

"You people are so extra. Who makes a mixtape for a six-hour drive?" She shook her head but put the CD in the player.

Taking one hand off the steering wheel, Sweets adjusted the volume. "I made mixtapes when I drove to college."

"That's different. You were driving from Georgia."

Sweets shrugged as the sound of a plucking guitar filled the small car followed by lyrics. *"I hopped off the plane at LAX..."*

"Oh, I love this song," said Sweets happily as Miley Cyrus's "Party in the USA" played loudly through the car's speakers.

Alba turned her head to look over her shoulder at Jax. "Are you serious? Miley Cyrus?"

"Yeah!" said Jax, bobbing her head to the music. "Isn't it the perfect song for a road trip?"

Alba rolled her eyes and pressed the skip button.

"Alba!" cried Jax. "What are you doing?!"

"I'm not listening to Miley Cyrus."

"B—"

The sound of a piano filled the car then as the next track started.

On the other side of Jax, Holly sucked in her breath. "Oh my gosh, I love this song."

"Right?" said Jax with a smile.

"What is this?" asked Alba.

"You don't know this song?" asked Sweets.

"Duh, duh, duh, duh..." sang Holly with the piano.

"No."

"*Making my way downtown, walking fast,*" sang everyone in the car except Alba and me.

I palmed my forehead. I was anything *but* a Vanessa Carlton fan.

Alba leaned forward and skipped the track. "Next!"

"Alba!" hollered Holly. "I liked that song!"

"Too bad. I'm not listening to that bubblegum pop junk."

The next song came on. "*Bye bye bye—*"

"'N Sync? Seriously, Shorty? What are you, twelve years old?" Alba pressed the eject button and pulled the CD out.

Jax sucked in her breath. "Alba! What are you doing?"

Alba rolled down her window and flicked the CD out onto the highway like she was throwing a frisbee. "Bye bye bye." Chuckling, she fluttered her fingers, waving at the CD as it caught on the breeze and hung in the air for a second before dropping to the pavement.

We all sat with our mouths gaping open for a long moment. Sweets was the first to speak.

"Alba!" Sweets pulled the car over to the side of the road. "That wasn't very nice."

"No, it wasn't!" agreed Jax. "That was so mean."

"Yeah, Alba. That was taking it too far. I mean, you could've just given Jax her CD back. You didn't have to throw it out the window."

"Are you serious, Red? She woulda just kept putting it in. Did you really wanna listen to that kiddie garbage?"

"I mean, maybe some Eagles or some Red Hot Chili Peppers would've been more my taste, but I wouldn't have thrown her CD out the window."

Now parked on the shoulder, Sweets pointed at the door. "You're getting it, Alba."

"I'm not getting it." Alba crossed her hands over her chest.

"Well, we're not leaving until you get her CD back." Sweets shut off the ignition and pulled the keys out.

Alba groaned and let her head fall back on the seat rest. "Ugh, fine." She pointed her finger backwards at the road and the CD magically lifted into the air and floated back towards the car and back inside her window. She handed it back to Jax. "Here."

Jax flipped it over to see little rock fragments stuck to the underside. "It's all scratched up!"

Alba shrugged. "Gee, sorry."

Jax's bottom lip plumped out. "You're not sorry, Alba. You're just plain old mean." She crossed her arms over her chest.

"Start the car, Sweets," instructed Alba. "We need to keep moving."

I glanced over at Jax. She was holding her breath. I knew her well enough to know that was her way of holding back tears. My eyes swung heavenward. *Ugh.* Now we were *all* going to have to pay for Alba's sins. Jax was going to be grumpy for the rest of the trip.

"Jax, what games did you bring?"

"None." Her voice was sharp. "Alba made me leave them all at the B&B."

"Liar. I know you. You brought something to play."

With her eyes closed, Jax lifted a shoulder.

I glanced over at Holly and cocked my head slightly towards Jax.

Holly got the message. "What'd you bring, Jax? I'll play."

"I'll play too," said Sweets.

"Alba will play too. Right, Alba?" I said, grabbing hold of her headrest and shaking it so it bounced her head off it.

"Red, quit."

I gave the headrest another shake. *"Right,* Alba?"

"Whatever."

Jax sighed and looked down at her bag. "Well, maybe I brought *one* game."

"Alright, then, let's see it."

She reached in her bag and pulled out a deck of cards.

"Would You Rather?" said Holly, reading the box. "What's that?"

Jax pulled the cards out. "Okay, I'm going to give each of you a scenario and you have to tell us what you'd rather do."

Alba squinched an eye. "How do you win?"

"You don't. It's just supposed to be a conversation starter." She plucked out the first card. "Okay, who wants to go first?"

"Ooooh, me!" said Holly, raising her hand.

Jax sniffled as she read the first card silently to herself. Her eyes brightened when she read the one she wanted to give to Holly. "Okay, I've got a good one for you, Holl. Would you rather be super hot physically but smell really bad, or would you rather be really ugly but smell irresistible?"

Holly's face scrunched up. "What kind of question is *that*?! Neither!"

I couldn't help but laugh. Jax had picked the perfect question for Holly.

Jax giggled. "You can't say neither. You have to pick one."

"That's a hard one, isn't it, Holly?" said Sweets.

"Yeah, it really is!" Holly swished her lips to the side. "I mean, what good does it do to be pretty if you smell so bad that boys don't want to get within twenty feet of you?"

"But if you smell irresistible, doesn't that mean that boys can't resist you?" I asked, trying to think out the question logically.

Holly shrugged. "I guess, but who wants to be ugly? I think I'd rather be pretty and smell bad. Maybe I can cover it up with perfume."

"Yeah, I think I'd pick that too," agreed Jax. "Okay, who's next?"

I raised my hand. "I'll go, Jax."

Jax squealed with excitement as she looked for a question for me. "Okay. I got it. Mercy, would you rather spend your teenage years alone in a room with only one other person, or would you rather spend the same time alone in a room with a really great computer and free Wi-Fi?"

I smiled. "Easy one. Computer and Wi-Fi."

Alba nodded. "Oh, for sure. I'd pick the same thing."

Sweets shook her head. "Oh, no way, not me. I'd have to have another human being. That's a really long time to be alone."

"Yeah, but what are you going to learn from that other person? Put me in a room for all those years alone with a computer and I'll learn to speak a dozen different languages. My magic skills would probably be better than they are now too, to be honest. I'd be super smart."

Holly furrowed her brows. "I couldn't go that long without a boy around."

"What's with you and boys? Why can't you be alone for that long, Holl? Why do you *always* have to have a boyfriend?"

She shrugged. "I don't know. It's just the way I'm wired,

I guess." She looked at me then. "Why don't you have to have a boyfriend?"

"Because I'm an independent woman," I said. "I don't need a boy to be happy."

"Speaking of boys, have you heard from Hugh since he left?" asked Sweets, glancing at me in her rearview mirror.

"He called me to tell me he made it home safe," I said with a shrug. "But I haven't heard from him since. He doesn't really text. He says his fingers are too fat. Plus his phone is ancient."

As if the phone gods had been waiting for their cue, someone's phone began to ring.

"Oh, that's me," said Holly brightly. "Hello?" There was a long pause and then Holly's eyes widened. "Oh, gosh. Okay. Yeah, no problem. No, no. I'll be careful with it. Yeah, I'll keep a close watch on it. Okay. Yeah, thanks. Bye."

"Who was that?" asked Jax.

"That was Abby, my dad's girlfriend. The one that sent me the box of clothes and stuff," said Holly. "Wow, she just told me that she accidentally sent me the wrong credit card."

"That black one?" asked Jax.

Holly's head bobbed. "Yeah, that one was meant for Dad. Dad told her to put the card that came in the mail in my package, but she didn't realize he'd ordered two new cards, one for me to use and the other one for him, and they both came on the same day. So she accidentally gave me the wrong one. The one she was *supposed* to give me had a two-thousand-dollar limit on it, but the one she gave me has no limit."

My jaw dropped. "The card she sent you has no limit?"

Holly nodded. "Yeah, and when Dad found out she sent the wrong card, he was really mad. He said it would be really bad if something happened to it because that's his business card. That could get him fired."

"Oh, man, that stinks. So can you still use it?"

"Yeah, Abby said just to use it for our absolute necessities."

Alba shook her head. "See? This is why it's bad to depend on other people. I'm gonna kill Tony for not mailing me the traveling money soon enough."

"Are you living in the dark ages, Alba? Who puts money in the *mail* anymore?" asked Holly. "Haven't you ever heard of Venmo?"

"Or Western Union," said Sweets. "That's how my dad sent me money that one time."

"Well, I don't bank anywhere in town, and Tony doesn't have time to be going to Western Union. Dad barely gives those boys time for lunch. He was just going to stick some cash in the mail. He must've forgotten to do it." She sighed.

Holly shrugged. "Well, it's not like Dad said I couldn't spend *anything*. We just can't spend *too* much."

Sweets smiled. "Don't worry. I have some money if we get in a bind."

We passed a sign that said Rest Stop Five Miles.

Sweets glanced up in her rearview mirror. "Hey, girls, do you mind if we stop at the next rest stop? I've been on my feet all day, and I'm exhausted. I need some caffeine and to use the restroom."

"Oh, I'll drive for you, Sweets," suggested Jax, lurching into the front seat again.

"Oh no. You're not driving, Shorty."

"Why can't I drive?" asked Jax, frowning.

"Because," said Alba tersely.

"Alba, geesh. Let the girl drive. She's bored," I said,

rolling my eyes. Even though I wouldn't say it out loud, I kind of liked the idea of Jax in the front seat.

"So?"

"So. Either let her drive or she's gonna make you play more games with us."

"Ugh," Alba groaned. She was quiet for a long moment until she finally sighed. "Oh, fine. You can drive. But I better not catch you putting any more stupid mixtapes in."

"Okay, but I get to control the radio," said Jax, clapping her hands excitedly.

"We'll see about that," grunted Alba.

CHAPTER 5

Thirty minutes later, armed with drinks, snacks, and the sandwiches Reign had packed for us, we all settled back into Sweets' car. With Jax driving and Sweets riding shotgun, I was forced to sit in the middle of the back-seat between Alba and Holly as a sort of human shield to keep the two of them from killing each other.

Jax happily grazed on chips, switching radio stations frequently as we drove through the mountains, where stations didn't come in well.

With some food in her belly, Alba became a little less hangry and actually loosened up enough to sing along with a few of the songs on the radio. Between random bouts of singing and laughing, we spent the next hour chatting about school and our classes for the upcoming year. Holly told us about her summer plans in California and how her mom thought she might be able to get her a bit part in a soap opera she was filming. Sweets told us that she was finally going to hire a new employee at the bakery to take the pressure off her a little bit. Alba admitted she was looking forward to getting to spend the summer with Tony.

And Jax and I complained about how boring the rest of the summer was going to be with Sweets working all day and Alba and Holly gone.

The five of us talked about where we might want to live during the next school year, and Sweets, Jax, and I all promised we'd do our best to find a decent place so we could be out of the B&B by the time school started.

In usual Holly fashion, she spent much of those first few hours texting someone and playing coy about which of her many boyfriends it was.

"I don't know why you just won't tell us," said Jax. "It's not like we're going to tell anyone."

"It's not about that," said Holly with an amused smile. "Sometimes you just want to keep things to yourself for a while."

"That makes absolutely *no* sense," said Alba. "You can't even keep your boobs to yourself. So what makes the name of the dude you're textin' so darn special?"

"Yeah, Holl. Not sure why we'd care who you're texting," I agreed. I swished my lips to the side as I stared at the road ahead. "Is it that one guy who lived down the hall from Hugh? The really broad-shouldered one? Because I thought he was kind of a jerk."

"Dan? No, I'm not texting Dan. He *was* a jerk."

I sighed. I was already tired of talking about Holly's constantly changing love life. I looked up at Jax. "Any changes in your magic abilities yet, Jax?"

Jax wiggled her nose and sniffled. "Nope. Nothing."

"Don't worry, Jaxie. It'll come," said Sweets.

"I sure hope so. I'm starting to wonder if I actually have any powers at all."

"Oh, quit, Jax. You do. You feel the tingle in your

fingers. It's just about focusing your energy. You'll figure it out at school in the fall," I said.

"*In the fall?!*" said Jax. "I can't wait until *the fall* to use my powers."

"Patience, Shorty. Patience. Good things come to those who wait," said Alba.

Jax frowned. "Yeah, I'm really not that good at patience."

"Yeah, we're all readily aware," I said with a smile.

We were all quiet for a little while. Finally, while eyeing the billboards on the side of the road, Jax broke the silence. "So how far are we driving tonight?" She pulled a tissue from the center console and held it to her mouth, stifling a sneeze.

Sweets yawned. "I'm ready for bed. So as far as I'm concerned, you can pull over whenever you get too tired to drive anymore, Jaxie."

"Oh, I'm not tired," said Jax. She held the tissue to her mouth again and held back another sneeze.

Sweets eyed her. "Are you getting sick, Jax?"

Jax used the tissue to blot her watery eyes. "No, I think this is just allergies."

"You better not get us all sick, Shorty."

"I'm not sick. It's allergies, I'm sure of it." Jax put on her blinker and switched lanes after driving around a slow-moving pickup truck. Glancing in her rearview mirror at us, she smiled. "So do you guys care where we stay tonight?"

"As far as I'm concerned, you can just drive all the way to Philly tonight. We'll find a place to stay there, and then in the morning we can do our sightseeing and take off for Jersey by lunchtime," said Alba.

"I just saw a sign," said Jax. "Philly's three more hours."

"Can you make it three more hours, Jax?" I asked, looking out into the quickly darkening sky.

"I can drive if you're too tired," said Alba. "I don't mind."

"Oh no," said Jax brightly. "I like driving. I just wish the radio stations came in better. They keep fuzzing out."

"Hey, Jaxie, can I use Emily and your blanket?" asked Sweets. "I need to catch up on my sleep."

"Oh, sure, Sweets. Mercy, can you pass those up here?"

I shoved both into the front seat.

Other than the radio fuzzing in and out, the car went quiet again. After about ten miles of silence, Alba finally put her jacket up against the car window. "Alright, well, I'm gonna take a little snoozer. Wake me up when we get there."

"Me too," said Holly. She snuggled up against my side and leaned her head on my shoulder.

Jax and I made eye contact through the rearview mirror. "You gonna nap too, Mercy?"

"No, Jax. I'll stay awake and keep you company."

She lifted a shoulder. "I'm fine. You can take a nap. I don't mind."

"But then who's gonna navigate?"

"The turnpike seems pretty self-explanatory," said Jax with a little giggle. "I don't think I can get lost."

"You sure?"

Jax nodded. "I'd rather have everyone in a good mood tomorrow. We have a lot of fun activities planned. So go ahead and take a nap. I've got the radio to keep me occupied."

"You're not gonna look at your phone while we're all sleeping, are you?"

Jax shook her head. "Two hands on the wheel, I swear."

An inadvertent yawn escaped my lips. "Okay. Well, then, I'll just take a little nap. Wake me up if you get sleepy, 'kay?"

Jax's head bobbed, and she smiled as she looked back at me in her mirror. "For sure. Night-night, Mercy."

"Night, Jax."

CHAPTER 6

I felt an arm drape across my waist.

My mouth, which had been hanging open, snapped shut. My mouth, tongue, and throat were all dry. I smacked my lips together a few times, moistening them.

With my eyes still closed, I sat there for a long moment, just processing. I heard nothing except the hum of the tires on pavement and Jax sniffling in the front seat. The radio was off now. I opened my right eye to see Alba was the one who had draped her arm across my waist. Her head was now on my shoulder.

I shut my right eye and opened my left eye and saw Holly was still leaning on my left shoulder.

Slowly, both eyes blinked open. It was pitch black outside. The only lights in the car came from the dash. I could almost make out Sweets, curled up on her side in the front seat.

"Hey, Jax, you okay?" I said from the backseat.

Jax's eyes swung up to look at me in her rearview mirror. "Hey, Mercy. Oh, yeah, I'm fine."

"What time is it?" I asked. I held up my wrist to look at my Batman watch, but it was too dark to see.

"Time?" asked Jax. Her squeaky voice was higher-pitched than usual.

"Yeah, it seems so dark outside."

"Umm, I think it's a little after midnight."

And then suddenly Alba bolted upright. "Midnight?! It's after midnight? And we're not there yet?"

Holly lifted her head groggily. "Where are we?"

"It's after midnight and we're still on the road," said Alba.

"We're still on the road?!" Holly said it like she was shocked.

"Welcome to planet earth, Cosmo. Yeah, we're still on the road. Does this look like a two-star motel to you?"

"Calm down, Alba," I said. "I'm sure we're almost there. Right, Jax?"

Sweets' arms lifted and ground into her eyes in the front seat.

"I think we have a little ways to go yet," said Jax.

"How in the world do we have a little ways to go, Shorty? We left Aspen Falls at six. We shoulda been to Philly an hour ago."

Sweets put her chair in the upright position and looked over at Jax. "Is this the turnpike? It looks different than the road we were on before."

"Well, I got off the turnpike," Jax admitted.

"You did what?!"

"What?"

"Jax! Why?"

"When?"

Our voices piled over the top of each other.

Jax flinched. "What?! Sorry! I got off the turnpike to get gas."

"Well, why didn't you get back on again?" asked Alba.

"I wanted to. I asked the guy at the counter how to get to Philadelphia and he said to take a right at the stop sign and then I'd see the sign for PA-283. So I did what he said and I ended up in Lancaster, and then I got completely turned around and confused."

"Well, why didn't you check your phone?" I asked.

"You said not to look at my phone while I'm driving!"

"Jax! You could've pulled over and checked it. Or you could've woken me up and I would've navigated."

"I didn't want to wake you guys. I thought I had everything under control. And I did check my phone at one point, but cell service isn't very good here."

"You could've gotten out the map!" said Alba.

"Alba, I can barely read a map when the sun is shining and I'm sitting at a table staring at it. You think I can read a map in the dark while I'm driving?"

Alba palmed her forehead. "Oh my gosh, Shorty. Why didn't you wake us up! Where in the world are we?"

Jax gnawed on her bottom lip. I could tell she was trying hard not to cry. "I don't know. I'm pretty sure we just passed a sign that said we're almost to Baltimore."

"Baltimore?! Maryland?!" hollered Alba.

"Maryland? What do you mean, Maryland?"

"It's a different *state*, Jax," I said, shaking my head. How had we all been so stupid as to let *Jax* drive us the last of the way to Philadelphia? "Baltimore is in Maryland."

Jax's eyes grew round. "Ohhhh, yeahhhhh. Baltimore, Maryland. I get it now." Her chin suddenly jerked forward. "Oh, wait. We're in Maryland?"

"Jax!" cried Holly. "How do you not know we're in Maryland?"

Jax shook her head. "I don't know, I guess I missed the sign."

"And it didn't occur to you that you don't go through Baltimore to get to Philadelphia?" I asked.

Jax shrugged. "I don't know. I don't ever *go* anywhere. How was I supposed to know that?"

"Oh, I don't know. Maybe because you learned it in elementary school geography," suggested Alba with a condescending shrug.

Sweets held her hands out. "Okay, okay. Relax. Everyone has a right to mess up once in a while."

"Yeah, well, Shorty's abusing the privilege," snapped Alba.

Sweets sighed. "Alba, it isn't all Jax's fault. Everyone fell asleep on her, including you. She didn't have anyone to navigate for her, so we can't blame it all on her."

"Thanks, Sweets," said Jax in a small voice. "I'm sorry, girls. I was trying to get us back on track. I guess I read the signs wrong, but I thought for sure I was going in the right direction."

My head rolled back on my neck. What a way to start our road trip.

"I can't believe this is really happening right now." Alba scooted forward in her seat and leaned around Sweets' seat to look at Jax. "You know what, Shorty? Pull over. I'm driving."

"Alba, I can drive. You just have to help navigate me back onto the turnpike."

"I don't even think we're near the turnpike anymore, Jax," said Sweets. "If we're almost to Baltimore, then we're way too far south."

I lifted my head and looked out the window. "Jax. Let's just pull over at the next truck stop. I have to go to the bathroom. We'll fill up the tank again, get some caffeine, check the map, and then Alba can drive us to Philly if she wants."

Defeated, Jax hung her head. "Oh, fine."

CHAPTER 7

I t was just after twelve thirty in the morning when we pulled up to the Dusty Trucker's Roadside Emporium, a truck stop off the Hereford, Maryland exit about a half hour north of Baltimore. There were no cars at the pumps, but there were several semitrucks parked on the east side of the building. When Sweets finished filling her tank with gas, we left the car parked in front of the pump and the five of us walked up to the building. Aside from two vehicles parked in front, a little red pickup truck, and a small older-model black van covered in rock band bumper stickers, the largest of which read *The Punk Heroes of Baltimore*, the place appeared to be dead.

A tall, husky older man with a beard, wearing a red baseball cap, exited the building as we entered and held the door for us. Each of us thanked him in turn as we filed past. Inside and to the right was a little greasy-spoon-style diner, and to the left was the convenience store and souvenir shop. A hallway with men's and women's bathrooms separated the diner and the convenience store and led to what I could only assume were the truck stop offices and storage rooms.

I stood with my back up against the tile wall as we each took turns waiting to use the bathroom. From where I stood, I could see into the diner and was surprised that even past midnight they were still serving customers. In one booth, a pair of truck drivers sat quietly, taking advantage of the advertised bottomless cup of coffee and the all-you-can-eat flapjacks. In another booth, a band of spiky-haired, tattooed punk rockers sat laughing and carrying on. They'd folded their napkins into paper footballs and were flicking them onto the table next to theirs.

When we'd all had a chance to use the restroom, we moved as a group into the convenience store to load up on caffeine for the rest of the trip. I fingered the little souvenirs on the wooden spinning rack and pondered whether or not my brother would want a *Don't Bother Me, I'm Crabby* shot glass or a 3-D crab-shaped pewter refrigerator magnet inscribed with the letters MD on the shell.

Just as I'd decided on the shot glass and put the magnet back on the rack, Jax came up behind me. "You getting yourself a souvenir?"

"I thought I should probably get Reign something, since he was nice enough to pack us those sandwiches."

"Aww, that's sweet. What are you getting him?"

I showed her the shot glass.

"Yeah, he'll like that. Maybe I'll get him something too. Do you like this magnet?" She picked up the crab I'd just put down.

"Yeah, I was debating between these two."

She nodded and then got a sudden funny look on her face.

I quirked a brow. "What?"

She held up a finger and I realized she was holding back a sneeze.

I nodded and began to walk away just as she let it loose. "Aaaachoo!" She swiped the back of her wrist across the bottom of her nose and sniffled.

"You better not get me sick, that's all I'm saying."

"Mercy! I'm not sick!" she insisted as I rounded the corner to look at the other side of the rack.

I'd just begun to look at a stand of folded t-shirts when Jax came wheeling around the corner. "Hey! Check this out." Smiling brightly, she showed me the magnet again.

The crab snapped its claws, extending them in my direction. I frowned. "Huh, I didn't realize it turned on. That's so cool."

"Yeah, I know, right? Reign's gonna love it."

I nodded, wishing I'd chosen the magnet for him after all. Now he was going to like Jax's present better than my present. I looked down at the t-shirts and debated whether to get him a Baltimore Ravens t-shirt instead of the shot glass.

Then Alba was behind me. "Hurry up, Red. We gotta go. It's late and I wanna go sit in the diner for a minute so we can spread the map out on the table and plan out our route to Philly."

"Alba, we have GPS," said Holly, joining in on the conversation.

"Obviously, GPS failed us," said Alba. "Just like I predicted it would. Now, I'm driving, and I chose to go old-school and get my directions off a map." She pointed at the restaurant. "I'll meet you guys in there."

"Okay, Jax and I have to pay for our stuff and then we'll be in."

Alba nodded. "Make it snappy. I don't wanna be up all night."

Holly and Alba headed for the diner, grabbing Sweets along the way. Jax and I walked up to the register together.

"Mercy, do you think the girls are mad at me because I got us lost?"

I lifted a shoulder. "Alba might be. But don't mind her. We know she gets mad at everything. It's just her personality. She doesn't really mean it."

"That'll be six fifty," said the woman behind the counter.

"Are you mad at me?"

I sighed as I slid the woman a ten-dollar bill. It was a catch-22. If I told Jax I was mad, she'd feel bad and be a pain in my butt for the rest of the trip. If I told her I wasn't mad, she'd never learn to quit doing things that annoyed me. But it was late. I decided to go with the lesser of two evils. "No, Jax. I'm not mad. I wish you would've woken us up, though. That would've saved us a bunch of time."

She hung her head. "I'm sorry."

"It's fine. What's done is done. Okay? Live and learn."

"Yeah," she whispered.

She paid for her crab, and the woman behind the counter wrapped it in paper and tucked it neatly into a souvenir bag. Both of us said thanks and then headed for the diner, where we discovered that the girls had already taken up residence in a corner booth.

Alba pointed at the map. "I think we're gonna get off here and head east," she said, her finger following the route she planned to take. "This'll take us to I-95 and into Philly."

"Hey, ladies, sorry for the wait. It's kinda been a one-man show this evening. What can I getcha?" asked a big burly fellow wearing a grungy white apron over a white t-shirt and black pants. He had shaggy brown hair that brushed the tops of his shoulders. His pudgy cheeks were red and glistened with sweat. As he stood looking at us, he used the bottom edge of his apron to mop the perspiration from his face.

By the look on her face, I could almost read Holly's disapproval in a thought bubble above her head.

"I'd take a large cup of coffee to go," said Alba.

"Just coffee?" he asked.

We all nodded.

"Yup. We won't be here long. Just needed to look at the map before we get back on the road."

That made him smile. "Oh, good. My waitress didn't show up for work, so I've been doing triple duty—waitress, cook, and dishwasher. But I can handle a cup of coffee."

"Ohhh, that stinks," said Jax.

"Yeah, it does," agreed Holly, wrinkling her nose. I was pretty sure she was talking about the odor emanating from the cook's body. I elbowed her in the ribs.

"I'll be right back with the coffee."

"Thanks."

I glanced up at the TV mounted in the corner of the room. The volume was muted, but the news was on and a close-up picture of an old man flashed up on the screen, followed by a picture of a rusted-out beige RV. "Can you tell how far away we are from Philly, Alba?"

"I don't know. Looks like it's about another two or two and a half hours."

"Two and a half hours?!" cried Holly. "Uh, that's *forever!*"

Alba pursed her lips as she folded the map back up. "You four are the ones that wanted to go on a road trip. Welp, you got your road trip. You can thank Shorty for this one."

"Alba, leave her alone."

Alba held her hands up in the air. "I'm just sayin'. Her little *accident* just cost us an extra tank of gas and three and a half hours."

"My dad's paying for the gas, Alba, so there's no reason to make Jax feel bad about that."

Alba scooted out of the booth. "Whatever. I'm gonna go pay for my coffee. I'll meet you morons in the car."

Shaking her head, Holly rolled her eyes. "Why do we even hang out with Alba?"

"Because she's smart," I said with a smile. "And she's better at magic than all of us combined."

"So? None of my friends in high school could do magic or were smart, and I was still friends with them," said Holly.

I laughed. "I'm not sure I'd be bragging about that. I sure hope you never said that to their faces."

Holly giggled. "Oh, trust me. It was no secret. They all knew it. I was the smart one in the group."

"Word to the wise, Holl. You should keep that nugget to yourself," I said with a half-smile. Giving that information to Alba would be like begging to be the butt of her next joke. I slid out of the booth as the girls laughed. "Come on. Let's go. We need to get back on the road."

"Ooooh! Shotgun!" cried Jax as she raced out the door ahead of all of us.

"Nuh-uh!" hollered Sweets. "It's my car. I've got shotgun."

"But I'm paying for gas," Holly pouted, chasing the two of them out the door.

I laughed and walked up to the counter. "Ready, Alba?"

"Yeah. Just waiting for my change."

"You sure you wanna drive? I don't mind driving."

"Nah, I'll drive. If you want something done right, you do it yourself."

"Thanks a lot."

"I'm just saying. We shouldn't have let Shorty drive in the first place."

"Yeah, well, we did. It is what it is. So we lose three hours of our lives that we can never get back. What else were we going to do with those three hours?" I asked her with a smile. I was trying to cheer her up.

"I don't know. We woulda been asleep."

My eyes swung towards the ceiling. "But you *were asleep*. So technically you didn't miss a thing."

She waved a hand at me. "Zip it, Red. I don't have time to argue."

"Argue?" I threw my hands up. "I wasn't trying to argue. I was trying to get that chip off your shoulder."

"Chip off my..." She stared at me hard then. "I *don't* have a chip on my shoulder."

"Ahhh, I think ya do. You've been grouchy this whole trip so far."

"Your point?"

"Oh, right. I meant *grouchier than usual* this trip."

"Look. I just wanna get home to my family. Is that so bad? You don't get it. You *live* with your mom and your brother. I haven't seen my folks or my brothers or my *husband* since Christmas."

I made a face. I really hadn't thought about it like that. Alba really never talked about her family much, so it never occurred to me that she might actually *miss* them. Alba was so tough that I never pictured her needing or missing *anybody*. "Oh, yeah. I guess that's true."

She nodded as she pocketed the change the cook handed her. "Thanks."

"Yeah, no problem," he said. "You girls drive safe."

We waved at him as we left the building.

"Yeah, so, that's why I really don't feel like sightseeing. I just wanna get home. Plus my brother's getting married. I've missed so much this year that I kinda wanna be a part of everything."

Suddenly I felt bad. I'd want to be a part of my brother's wedding-day preparation plans too if he were getting married. "Ugh. Why didn't you just say that before, Alba?"

"Say what? That I'm a big loser that wants to see her mommy and daddy?"

I chuckled. "Yeah. You could've. We would've gotten it then. The girls and I could've just done our sightseeing on the way home."

"I tried to tell you," she countered.

"Yeah, well, your bedside manner leaves a lot to be desired."

"That's just how I am, Red. I don't have a sweet side."

"Yeah, you do. I've seen it. We've all seen it. But it's like a Sasquatch sighting. It's rare, and when we finally see it, we're so stunned, all we can do is stare and point."

She elbowed me. "You're a nut, Red."

I laughed. "Takes one to know one, Alba."

She rolled her eyes. "Oh my gosh. You learn that in the first grade?"

"You know what they say, everything I need to know I learned in kindergarten." Finally to the car now, I peered in through the window. Holly was in the front passenger seat, and Jax and Sweets were in the back. "Who says you get shotgun, Holly?"

She grinned and waved her father's black card in the air. "Daddy does."

I rolled my eyes and opened the back door. "Scooch over, Jax."

Instead of sliding over, Jax hopped out of the vehicle. "I called the seat by the door. You're in the middle."

"But you're the smallest. You should be in the middle."

"I was in the middle for the first shift."

"I was in the middle for the second shift. It's not my turn to be in the middle again."

Jax shrugged. "You got to sleep for the last four hours. It's my turn to nap, and I got out here first so I could pick my seat. Sorry, Mercy."

I groaned and climbed inside as Alba opened up the driver's-side door and sat down too. She took a sip of her coffee before belting herself in.

"Are we ready?" she asked.

"All ready, Captain," said Jax with a giggle.

"Keys," she said, holding her flattened palm out.

"Oh, sorry." Jax pulled the keys out of her jacket pocket and handed them to Alba.

Alba put the keys in the ignition. "Philly or bust," she said before trying to start the engine.

The car made a whirling sound, but the engine didn't turn over.

"What the—"

Sweets sat forward and looked over Alba's shoulder. "What happened? Why's it making that noise?"

Alba shook her head and tried to start it again, but it made the same sound. "It's not starting."

CHAPTER 8

"What?! Why isn't it starting?" asked Sweets.

Alba tried to start it a third time and got the same result. "I don't know, but if I had to guess, I'd say it's a clogged fuel filter." She slammed her hand into the steering wheel. "Uh! Are you kidding me right now?! See, Sweets? I *told* you we should have had it changed before we left."

Sweets' brows lifted and she sat back in her seat, mouth pinched shut.

"Can't you just go buy a new one inside?" asked Holly, her nose wrinkled.

Alba looked over at Holly. "Maybe, but do you think *I'm* going to change it?"

"I don't know. Are you?"

"No! I have no idea how to change a fuel filter. Do you?"

"Eww, of course not."

"Well, then, why would you assume that *I* know how to change a fuel filter?"

Holly flipped her blond hair over her shoulder and

shrugged. "I don't know. Because you're from New Jersey?"

That made Alba swivel around in her seat. "I'm sorry. Do you think that's a class taught in the public schools there or something?"

"I don't know, Alba!" Holly hollered back. "I don't know your life."

"No, you *don't* know my life. So don't *assume* I know how to fix cars. I only know that a clogged fuel filter will make your car not start properly because it happened to Pop's moving truck once when I was with him. But *I* didn't go fix it. We took it to the shop, and *they* fixed it."

"Well, we're witches," I said. "There's gotta be something we can do to fix it."

Alba looked at me through her mirror. "You take magical automotives last semester and forget to mention it to me, Red?"

I rolled my eyes. "Of course not. But can't we, like, say a spell and get it moving again?"

"I'm sure there's a spell out there. I just don't happen to know it," said Alba. "Anyone pack a spell book?"

The car fell silent.

She pursed her lips and nodded. "I figured."

"So then what do we do?" asked Jax.

With a grunt, Alba let her head fall forward into her hands.

"I don't know, Jax," I whispered out the side of my mouth. I was a little afraid of Alba blowing up even more, and I hoped Jax was smart enough just to be quiet while we all took in what was happening. Our car had broken down. It was almost one a.m. and we were at a truck stop off the interstate, almost three hours away from our intended destination and just as far from home. What were we going to do?

"Maybe they have mechanics here," said Holly with a shrug.

"Yeah, maybe," said Jax. She opened her door. "Come on, Holly, let's go inside and ask."

Holly sighed but got out of the vehicle with Jax. The two of them linked arms and ran back into the truck stop.

Sweets and I looked at each other uncomfortably as we waited for the girls to come back. Alba was still bowed forward with her head in her hands. I knew she was angry but was fighting hard to keep from blowing up, which I appreciated.

Finally, we saw the door open and Holly and Jax burst out. They ran towards the car and scrambled inside.

"They have a mechanic!" said Jax excitedly.

Alba's head popped up. "Get out. They do?"

Holly nodded. "His name is Phil and he gets here at eight a.m."

Alba's head fell back against the seat rest. "That's in seven hours!"

"Congratulations, you win the subtraction award of the day, Alba," cracked Holly.

Alba swiveled sideways in a flash. "You want a piece of me, Cosmo?"

Reflexively, I lunged forward between the seats, keeping the two of them apart. "Okay, okay," I said. "Alba, she was just giving you what you *always* give to her. Don't dish it if you can't take it."

"Yeah, well, I'm not in the mood for her bull."

"You think she's *ever* in the mood for yours?" I countered. "Now, the two of you just need to knock it off. We're all tired. We're all grumpy and upset because the car won't start. But it looks like we're sticking around until morning." I looked back at Jax. "Jax, did you guys ask if they have any motels around that we could stay at tonight?"

"Yeah, they have one about five miles ahead," said Holly. "But the guy in the diner said we were welcome to hang out in there until morning."

"I'm not sleeping in a diner all night," said Alba.

"Well, unless you packed five broomsticks, I think that's our only choice for the night," said Holly.

"We could ask one of those truck drivers in there to give us a ride," suggested Jax. "Or those punk rocker kids."

Alba blew air out her nose. "We are *not* hitching a ride. Are you *crazy*?" She shook her head. "You know what? Don't answer that. I already know the answer."

"Alba. Insulting the girls is not going to help this situation. Now, I know you're upset. You wanted to get home to your family. I get it. We all want to get moving too. But this is the hand that we were dealt. I'm making the executive decision. Grab your stuff, girls. We're staying in the diner until morning. Then we'll get the car in to get fixed, and as soon as it's ready we'll take off for Jersey City."

"Jersey City!" cried Sweets, Holly, and Jax simultaneously.

"Yes. Alba wants to get back to her family. She hasn't seen them since Christmas. Can we blame her?"

I looked around the car. Everyone had their eyes down in their laps. "Okay. Exactly. We'll drop her off, and then the rest of us can drive down to Philly on our way home."

"But I have to be back on Tuesday!" said Sweets.

"We'll be back to Aspen Falls by Tuesday."

Alba pulled the keys out of the ignition. "Oh, fine. We'll stay here until the car is fixed. Everyone, grab your stuff."

~

Rick, the diner cook that had waited on us, turned out to be a fairly nice guy, albeit pretty greasy. He allowed us to take up residence in three of his booths until the mechanic's shop opened at eight.

Since Jax was the only one who hadn't napped, she was the first to fall asleep on her padded seat. She curled up into a ball with Emily and was out like a light within the first ten minutes.

Sweets shared the booth with Jax, and it didn't take long before she was out too. Alba and I shared the middle booth, and Holly insisted on having her own booth because she needed enough room to spread her facial things out. Of course she'd thrown a temper tantrum because Alba had refused to let her get her big bag down off the top of the car —her reason being that we didn't want to have to take the time to tie everything back up there in the morning when our car was fixed—so Holly had to sleep in the clothes she'd worn that day and she was none too excited about it.

With Sweets and Jax asleep and Holly working on her beauty regimen, I finally looked over at Alba, who was across the table from me. We were both backed up to the wall behind us and had our legs extended out on the booth in front of us. "We'll be to Jersey City by noon, Alba. Don't stress, alright?"

"Easy for you to say," she muttered.

I made a face. "How is it easy for me to say?"

"You're not in a hurry. I'm the one that's trying to make it to my brother's wedding."

"Alba, your brother's wedding is on Monday. It's Saturday. You've got plenty of time."

"Well, I'd like to be there early."

"I know," I said, slinking down into my seat. "We're gonna get you home by noon tomorrow. Don't worry." I yawned. "I mean, what else could possibly go wrong?"

CHAPTER 9

"Hey girls, I just saw Phil pull into the parking lot," said a voice from somewhere far away. "You hear me? The mechanic's here."

My eyes fluttered open, and I glanced over to see that Alba was gone. I looked to my right to see Sweets slowly rising. Jax was still curled up in a ball on her seat. I looked to the other side and saw Holly was still knocked out in her booth.

"Thanks, Rick," I said, yawning. I ground the sleep out of my eyes. "Hey, Sweets, you seen Alba?"

"No, I just woke up."

"Me too." My back hurt from sleeping in such a jacked-up way. I rubbed the kink out of my neck as I slid out of the booth. "I'm gonna go use the bathroom."

"Okay, I'll wake the girls up," said Sweets.

I nodded and went to the bathroom. It was locked. Seconds later, Alba popped out.

"Morning, Alba."

"Hey, Red."

"Rick said Phil's here."

"The mechanic?"

I nodded.

Alba rushed towards the diner.

Before leaving the bathroom, I splashed some cold water on my face and rebraided my wild hair. I wished I had my toothbrush, but it was in the bag on top of the car with the rest of my stuff. I wondered if I could just get a hand inside my bag without having to untie everything. I walked back to the diner. Alba was nowhere to be found. Holly and Jax were just beginning to wake up.

"Where's Alba?"

Sweets pointed towards the parking lot. "She went to go talk to the mechanic."

I peered out the window and saw Alba walking. "I'm gonna go with her."

"Okay. You want me to order you any breakfast?"

"It's okay. I'll get something when I come back in." I rushed outside and caught up to Alba, who was walking towards a junker truck parked around the side of the building.

"Excuse me, are you Phil?" Alba asked a tall, skinny guy wearing denim coveralls and brown work boots and pulling a brown cooler from the truck.

The man nodded. "Yup."

"Our car broke down and we're in a hurry to get it fixed again. You got any time this morning to take a look at it?"

"I can take a look. Might not have the parts I need today."

"I think it's a fuel filter," said Alba.

"Where's the car?"

"Other side of the building," said Alba, pointing. After it hadn't started, we'd had to put it in neutral and push it around to a parking spot so it didn't block any pumps.

"I'll meet you over there," said Phil. "Just gotta unlock the shop and put my stuff away."

Alba and I turned and started back towards the car. "Let's hope he's got the right parts," she mumbled under her breath.

When we rounded the corner to where we'd parked the car, I sucked in my breath. "Alba!"

She looked over at me, her eyes wide. "Jeez, Red. You scared me. What?!"

My mouth gaped as I pointed at the car. "Look!"

Following my finger, her brow furrowed in confusion. "What am I looking at?"

"All of our stuff! It's gone!"

CHAPTER 10

After running back in the diner to get the girls, the five of us stood on the pavement, staring at the car in shock. It was as if we were wondering if perhaps our bags would magically reappear if we stared long enough. But when Phil showed up with his tow truck to drag the car around to the other side of the building, where his shop was located, we were forced to realize that our tie-downs had all been severed and everything that had been on top of the car was truly gone.

As the one that had lost the most, Holly's mouth gaped open. "How can it all be gone?"

I perched a crooked elbow on her shoulder. "That sucks, Holl. I mean, I know I lost some stuff too, but it was literally just a few t-shirts and my toothbrush."

"That was every single outfit my dad sent me," she whispered sadly. Tears welled up in her eyes. "I didn't get to wear a single thing."

"You got plenty of clothes anyway, Cosmo. You didn't need all that," said Alba.

"Yes, I did! My *dad* sent that to me. Who *steals* another

woman's clothes? And why? It's not like they'll appreciate them like I would have."

"Why does anyone steal anything?" I said. "They didn't know what was in the bags, I'm sure."

"They had to assume it was clothes. What else do you put in suitcases?"

I shrugged. "I don't know. Jewelry. Cash. Electronics?"

Holly sucked in her breath then. "My jewelry! I didn't have time to decide what jewelry went with my new clothes, so I just packed it all! All my jewelry was in that bag!"

Alba frowned. "I told you not to pack so much. If you'd brought a smaller bag, then you wouldn't have lost so much."

Holly spun on her heel and wagged a finger in Alba's direction. "This is all *your* fault."

Alba's eyes widened as she pressed her fingers to her chest. "*My* fault? How is this *my* fault?"

"*I* wanted to bring it all inside. *You* wouldn't let me!"

"I was the one that told you to leave all that crap home in the first place. If you woulda listened to *me*, there wouldn't have been anything to tie to the roof because we coulda jammed it all in the trunk."

I stepped between them and held a hand up separating them. "Okay, okay. Fighting is only going to make this trip worse than it already is. What's done is done. Holly, I'm sorry about your clothes. I lost stuff too, and so did Jax. It's not the end of the world."

Standing next to me, Jax hugged Emily tightly to her chest. "I'm just thankful I had Emily with me inside."

"See!" cried Holly. "You guys didn't lose anything *really* valuable. I did. We have to see if the convenience store owner will let us check their security tapes. We have to get my stuff back."

Alba shook her head. "Oh no. We don't have time to be playing clothes detective. We have to get to New Jersey by noon."

"By noon?!" said Holly. "No, no. We need to find whoever stole my clothes and track them down. *Then* we can go to New Jersey."

Alba crooked a brow and looked around. "Am I the only one who hears how stupid she sounds right now?"

"Alba," chided Sweets. "Be nice. Holly just lost everything her dad gave her."

"No, she didn't. Her dad gives her everything. He probably gave her the clothes she's wearing right now!"

Holly looked down at her outfit. "No, he didn't. I ordered this outfit online."

"Yeah, well, whose account did you charge it to?"

Holly's lips pressed together into a firm line.

Alba threw her hands up as if she'd proven her point. "See?"

Holly shot forward, her finger pointed at Alba. "That's different! This time he didn't just pay the bill. This time he picked those clothes out for me!"

"Bull," spat Alba. "His girlfriend picked them out for you. Your dad probably didn't even know what she sent you."

This was getting out of hand. "Okay, okay, okay. Alba. Holly. Relax. You too are stressing me out."

Sweets and Jax chimed in next. "Me too."

"Me three."

I looked at Holly. "Now look, Holl. We all feel bad for you. And it sucks for Jax and me, too. We don't have any clothes to change into either, but I know in the grand scheme of life, it's not the end of the world. Okay? And be thankful you had your makeup in the bag you brought in last night, so that's a positive. How about for the sake of this trip and the sake of our sanity, we just focus on getting the car fixed and then getting on our way, okay?"

I knew Holly didn't want to let it go. She wanted to go to the ends of the earth to track down her stolen items, but she also knew it was four against one. We all wanted to get moving.

She sighed. "Fine."

My head bobbed. "Good. Now let's go inside and get our stuff together. We can have a little breakfast and then find out how long it's going to take for Phil to fix our car. Okay?"

When Holly wasn't quick to move, Sweets put her arm around her shoulder. "Come on, Holly. Let's make the best of a bad situation. They've got some amazing-looking caramel rolls in their bakery case. Let's go get something to eat. We'll all feel better with food in our bellies."

Reluctantly, she let the group lead her inside.

LINED up at the diner's counter, Rick set each of us girls up with a caramel nut roll, a glass of milk, and a bottomless cup of coffee. Ingesting the food and caffeine made me feel slightly more human than I had before. I hadn't slept well in the wee hours of the morning, and my neck still hurt from the awkward way I'd had to lie all night. Plus I didn't have a toothbrush, and I was feeling pretty greasy. I made a mental note right then and there to check the truck stop's personal hygiene section after breakfast and see if they sold toothbrushes and maybe even a stick of deodorant.

As we ate, a radio chattered in the background, advising the local listening area of the forecast for the weekend, while a TV flickered in the corner replaying the same close-up picture of an old man and an RV that it had earlier. With the volume off, I still couldn't hear what the man had done to deserve an encore appearance on the news.

None of us girls spoke as we ate, and we were all still groggy and lost in our own thoughts when Rick came to offer us all refills on our coffee. Alba was the first to speak.

"No thanks, Rick. We need to go see how Phil's doing on our car. We'll just take the check."

"Sure thing." He nodded and put the coffee carafe down and went to his register while I went back to my booth to make sure I hadn't forgotten anything.

Holly, Jax, and Sweets followed me.

Jax grabbed her blanket from her booth and wrapped it around her shoulders. "They've got the air conditioner high in here," she said, sniffling.

"Your cold is getting worse, isn't it?" I asked her as I pulled my own sweatshirt on.

She wiggled her nose. "I wouldn't say worse. It's just not getting any better."

Holly packed all of her makeup back into her makeup bag and shoved it into the backpack she'd had as her one personal item in the car.

With the bill in her hand now, Alba rejoined us at our booths. "Are we splitting the bill?"

Holly groaned. "Ugh, no. I'll just give you my dad's card. Hang on, let me get my purse." She pulled her backpack up on the table and dug through it, in search of her purse.

"I can pay some too," said Sweets.

"No, I got it, Sweets." Holly frowned as she spoke the

words. Looking concerned, she lifted up her backpack and looked on both sides of the booth's seat cushions. Then she looked under the booths.

"What are you looking for?" I asked.

"My purse. I thought it was in my backpack."

"You lost your purse?" asked Alba.

"I didn't *lose* my purse," snapped Holly. "It was right there when we went to sleep." She pointed at the other side of the booth.

"You left your purse on the opposite side of the booth from you?"

"Yeah, why?"

"Because someone might have stolen it, that's why. If you'd have slept with it on your side, then it would've been safer."

"No one stole it, Alba, it must have dropped out when I got my makeup out this morning."

"Maybe you left it in the bathroom, Holly," suggested Jax with a shrug.

"Go check for her, will ya, Shorty?"

Jax took off like a shot for the bathroom while Holly, Sweets, Alba, and I all scoured the area for Holly's purse.

"It's not in there," said Jax.

"And I don't see it anywhere around here either," said Sweets.

"Maybe you forgot you left it in the car," I suggested.

"No, I'm sure I didn't forget. But I guess we can check."

Sweets walked over to Alba and took the check. "I'll pay for breakfast." She sat her purse down on the table and opened it. She reached inside to grab her wallet out and then almost immediately turned her purse upside down to dump out the contents. "Girls! My wallet's not in here."

"What?!" asked Alba.

"My wallet. It's not in here!" cried Sweets.

"You gotta be kiddin'."

Sweets' head shook rapidly as tears filled her eyes. "No. It's gone!"

I held out two hands to calm her. "Relax, Sweets. Maybe you left your wallet in the car too. We'll go check." I reached into my back pocket and pulled out the last of the cash I'd brought with me for the trip. I didn't have a lot of money to my name as a broke college student, but I had what little I had left of the tips I'd made working at the B&B. "I'll take care of breakfast."

CHAPTER 11

Phil's shop was outside around the west side of the building. Tires, rims, and old fenders littered the pavement north of the building. The overhead garage door was wide open, and we noticed that Phil already had Sweets' car up on his lift and was underneath.

"Hey, Phil, we need to check the car for our wallets," said Alba.

Phil emerged from beneath the car. He wiped his hands on a shop rag and lowered the car. Holly, Sweets, and Jax made a beeline for the car while Alba and I stayed back to chat with Phil.

"So, do you have any idea what's wrong with it yet?"

"I have a feeling it's the fuel pump," he said.

"The fuel pump!" Alba's eyes went wide. "You have to be kiddin' me! I thought it was just going to be a clogged fuel filter."

"Well, I haven't had time to run any diagnostic tests yet, but I'm pretty sure that's what it's gonna show."

"How much is that going to cost?" I asked.

"Well, the parts is what's gonna kill ya. Parts stores

around here charge extra to deliver on the weekends. I'd say between a new fuel pump and labor, you're talking around eight hundred."

My eyes widened. "Dollars?!"

"No, eight hundred fish sticks, Red. Of course dollars," snapped Alba. "How long's it going to take to fix?"

"If I get the part ordered by nine, I think the parts store I order through in Baltimore can have it here to us by ten or eleven at the latest depending on their volume this morning. I could possibly have it in for you by close of business today."

It was Alba's turn to freak out. "Close of business today! What are we supposed to do until then?"

Phil cracked a smile. "Rick's got all-you-can-eat flapjacks inside. My suggestion? Get your money's worth."

Feeling defeated, Alba and I walked back over to the girls.

"Well?" I said. "Find your wallets?"

Jax was the first one to pull her head back out of the vehicle. With her face scrunched up, she shook her head sadly.

My body crumpled inwardly. "You're kidding?"

"No, I wish I was," she said.

"Okay, ladies, if you want me to get back to work on your vehicle, I'm going to need to keep moving on it. I need to have parts ordered within the next half hour."

"Holly, Sweets, come on," I said. "Phil needs to work on the car."

Reluctantly, Sweets and Holly crawled out of the vehicle, and the five of us met just outside the shop.

"I don't know what happened," whispered Holly sadly.

"What happened is we got robbed," said Alba. "Someone probably saw us sleeping in the diner. They got their hands on whatever wallets they could, then they saw our vehicle, knew it was ours and that we were passed out cold. It was like taking candy from a baby."

"So if we don't have any money, how are we gonna pay Phil?" I asked. "I mean, after paying for breakfast, I've got like thirty bucks left."

Jax winced. "I've got forty-five."

"And I've got a little cash too, but not near enough to pay for a tank of gas, let alone to pay Phil," said Alba.

"How much is it going to be?" asked Sweets.

"He thought eight hundred."

"Dollars?!" she gasped.

"No, fish sticks," I said with one raised eyebrow and a half-smile.

"That's not funny, Mercy," she said, her brow furrowed. "That's something Alba would say."

"She did say it!" I laughed. "Look, I know this seems bad. Really, really bad. We don't have any money. We don't have a working car. We were robbed. We're out in the middle of nowhere."

Holly palmed her forehead. "Oh my gosh. Girls, it just occurred to me that my dad's black card was in my purse."

"You're just now realizing that, genius?" asked Alba.

"Noooo, I mean, I realized it before, but I guess it just hit me. Like, he's gonna *kill* me. I was supposed to be extra responsible for that card, and now it's gone."

"You should call him and tell him what happened so he can cancel it," I said.

"Call him and tell him I lost his black card?" Holly shook her head, her eyes wide. "Are you *kidding* me? No way! He'll never give me another card again if I tell him I lost it and all the clothes he sent me."

"I'd think he'd be even more mad if whoever stole it charges a bunch of stuff to it," said Sweets.

Holly nodded, her eyes now looking crazed. "Which is *exactly* why we have to get the card back."

"Get it back?" I said. "We don't even know who has it. How are we supposed to get it back?"

"We'll look at the security tapes like I suggested in the first place."

"What good's that going to do us?" asked Alba. "Even if we know who stole the stuff, how are we supposed to find them? We have no car!"

Holly's face fell. "Ugh."

"Okay, girls. For starters, we need to figure out how we're going to pay for the car to get fixed. Then we'll discuss what to do about the credit card." I started walking back towards the building. "Come on. Let's go see if Rick minds if we take our booths back. We need to figure out how to come up with some quick cash."

CHAPTER 12

"I could call my brother and see if he can't Western Union me some money," I suggested with a shrug.

"I already asked at the counter," said Alba. "They don't do Western Union here."

"Besides, Reign's phone's not working right now," said Holly, frowning.

Alba lowered her brows and looked at Holly curiously. "How do you know, Cosmo?"

Jax piped up. "Don't you remember, Alba? Reign told us before we left he was going into the mountains for the weekend, and he'd have a bad cell signal. That's how she knows. Right Holly?"

Holly's mouth curled into a smile. "Oh, yup. Exactly."

"Ugh, great." I let my head fall into my hands.

"Well, why don't we call Aunt Linda and see if she can pay Phil with a credit card over the phone?" suggested Jax with a shrug.

I sighed. I hated the idea of asking my mom for that kind of money. She'd already did so much for me and my friends, and I hated the idea of being a further mooch. But I felt like I didn't have a lot of choice. "Fine. I'll call her." I pulled my phone out and dialed the number to the B&B. It rang about ten times before someone finally answered.

"Habernackle's," said a cheery, but breathless, voice. It was the new girl my mom had hired. I could hear the usual morning rush in the background.

"Hey Sam, this is Mercy. Can I talk to my mom quick?"

"Well, she's kind of busy right now. Can I have her call you back?"

"It's kind of important. I don't mind holding."

"Okay, I'll tell her you're on the phone."

I waited for a solid three minutes, staring at the girls and drumming my fingers on the table.

When Mom finally picked up the phone, she was as breathless as Sam had been. "Mercy, this isn't a good time right now. Sam and I are swamped without you and Reign."

"But Mom…"

"Is everyone okay?" she cut in.

"Well, yeah…"

"No one's bleeding?"

"No."

"Then I'll talk to you on Monday when you get back. Love you Mercy Bear." The phone went dead.

I sighed and looked at the girls. "Mom's busy."

"You can call her later?" suggested Sweets.

I shook my head. "I feel too guilty. Her and Sam are getting slammed at the B&B right now. Reign's not there, Jax and I aren't there…"

Shaking her head, Alba swiped a hand in the air. "I agree with Red. Linda's done enough for us. We can figure this out on our own."

"Maybe you can call your dad, Holly," suggested Jax.

Holly's eyes went big. "Oh no! And admit that I lost his black card?" She shook her head wildly. "Are you nuts? He'd kill me. No. No. That's not happening."

"Well, I'd call my mom and dad, but I know they don't have that kind of money," said Sweets sadly.

"Oh, I know. We could ask Phil if he'd let us mail him a check when we get back to Aspen Falls," suggested Jax.

"Jax, Phil's not gonna give us our car back until we pay him. If we don't get our car back, then we have no way to make it to Aspen Falls," I explained as patiently as I could.

"Well, we could *ask him* if he'd let us have our car back and then we can mail him a check."

Alba shook her head. "Ohhh, no. We aren't saying a word about this to Phil. The second he finds out that we don't have any money, he's gonna stop working on the car."

Sweets frowned. "Well this just stinks. If they hadn't stolen my purse I could've paid Phil myself. I should have enough money in my account to cover the repair bill."

Holly looked at me curiously. "Don't you have a credit card or something, Mercy?"

I let out a little puff of air. "Puh, me? Who would trust *me* with a credit card?"

"A debit card would work, then maybe Sweets could call her bank and transfer some money into your account or something," said Holly.

"No, I had a checking account once, when I was in high school and my mom made me get a job. I never balanced my account, and then I'd run out of money." I shook my head. "It was dumb. I'd just rather carry cash. Then I know exactly how much money I have at all times."

Alba nodded. "That's how I do it too. My pops has always said, cash is king."

"Well, I have a checking account and a debit card," said Jax brightly.

"You do? Maybe Sweets can transfer some money into your account, then." Holly looked hopeful.

Jax smiled sheepishly. "Oh, well, I didn't *bring* it. I just brought some cash. I didn't want to overspend. I thought if I had my debit card, I'd be tempted to spend too much."

"Ugh, then why'd you even say anything?" asked Alba.

Jax's face got long. "I don't know. You were all talking about it. I just thought we were sharing stories."

"No, Jax. We're trying to figure out a way to come up with the money to fix Sweets' car," I barked. My patience was running low.

"Oh. Well, why don't we see if Rick could use our help? He said his waitress quit. Maybe we could wait tables for some cash."

"There's no way Rick's gonna pay us eight hundred dollars to wait a few tables for one day's work," said Alba.

I shrugged. "You'd be surprised, Alba. I made over a hundred dollars in tips waiting breakfast tables at the B&B one day."

"Yeah, but the B&B is actually *busy*. This place is deader than a zombie apocalypse," said Alba.

"What other choice do we have?"

"We could split up," said Sweets. "I'll offer to cook for him. Mercy and Jax could wait tables. Maybe they could use their bathrooms cleaned or something on the convenience store side."

"Oh, I know what I could do," said Holly, raising her hand excitedly. "I could do psychic readings and fortune tellings outside. I bet that will bring in a lot of tip money. They probably don't have a lot of psychics around here."

I sighed. "I mean, it's worth a try. What other options do

we have?" I looked over at Alba. She looked like she'd just eaten and her meal was threatening to come back up on her. "What do you think, Alba?"

"I think there's no way we're coming up with eight hundred in one day. Even if there are five of us."

"Well, we have a little cash too. How much do you have?" I asked.

She pulled her cash out and counted it out on the table. "Thirty-seven dollars."

"And I've got thirty," I said. "Jax, what do you have left for cash?"

She pulled a wad of cash out of her stuffed unicorn's back pocket. "I've got forty-five."

"Okay, well, that's a hundred twelve," I said, adding it up in my head. "So we're short just under seven hundred."

"Plus we need money to eat and for gas," said Sweets.

"All we need is enough gas to get to Jersey," said Alba with a nod. "I can get enough money from Tony to send you back to Aspen Falls."

"Plus we have to track down the people who stole my dad's credit card," said Holly. "And my clothes!"

"We're never going to find them, Holly," I said with a sigh. "You just need to call your dad and have him cancel it."

"But he's gonna kill me!"

I shook my head. "Then you should have been more careful with it. You're just going to have to take whatever's coming to you."

Holly plumped out her bottom lip. I could tell she wasn't willing to accept defeat yet. "We'll see. I just need a little bit of time to figure out what to do."

"Suit yourself." I looked around the table. We all looked tired and defeated, but if we ever wanted to get out of the truck stop we were stranded at, we needed to band together. "Okay girls. This is it. We need to make seven hundred dollars in the next eight hours. Can we do it?"

"Mm," said Sweets, lifting a shoulder. "Maybe."

"Probably not," answered Alba.

Jax grinned from ear to ear. "I'll do my best!"

"Me too," agreed Holly.

I shook my head. "Okay, I'm gonna need a little more enthusiasm than that. Girls. *I said*, Can we do it?"

Jax threw out her thumb. "Yes, we can!"

"What she said," said Holly.

"Yeah," agreed Sweets with a giggle. "What she said."

"Oh, come on, Alba. Can we do it?"

"Since when did you become so annoyingly perky?"

"I don't know. Since our car broke down and I have no choice. Come on. Help me out here. Can we do it?"

"Sure, why not?"

CHAPTER 13

Working at the diner that day turned out to be one of those good news, bad news deals.

The good news had been that Rick was more than excited when we'd made him our offer to work for the rest of the day to earn money towards getting our car fixed. He admitted that he'd pulled a double shift when his waitress had quit, and since she was scheduled to work Saturday too, he'd been debating between either closing for the afternoon so he could run home and catch some zzz's or pulling a triple shift. In the end, he'd agreed to let Sweets cook and Jax and me wait tables, and he'd decided to sleep on a cot in the storage room while we ran the place. That way he wouldn't be far away if we needed anything.

The bad news was that, aside from the truckers who stopped for a cheap plate of food and a few cups of coffee, the place was pretty dead.

For their parts, Alba and Holly spoke to Dallas Hartman, the truck stop manager. Alba asked if they needed any help, and she'd actually managed to score a job unloading and putting away a supplies truck in the back. With her telekinetic abilities, I knew she'd be done with the job by lunchtime and might even have time to stock shelves.

Holly, on the other hand, had gotten permission to set up a folding table in the front of the building and hang a sign offering psychic readings and fortune tellings for twenty dollars a pop, tips welcome. It was my hope that she'd be able to rake in a fortune doing it.

At about a quarter after eleven, Jax hopped up on a barstool and gave it a spin. When she stopped spinning, she sniffled and wiggled her nose. "Mercy! It is sooo dead in here. How are we ever going to make eight hundred bucks if it's so dead?"

I couldn't bring myself to tell her that I was worried about the exact same thing. What good would it do anyone if we both became whiners? "Positive thoughts, Jax, positive thoughts."

"Fine. I'm *positive* we're not going to make eight hundred bucks if it keeps up like this," she complained.

I sighed. "Maybe Holly's having better luck than we are. I'm gonna check on her. Why don't you see if those guys over there need any more coffee?"

Jax frowned as she slumped forward on her seat. "I just asked them. I think they're sick of me hovering."

"Then do something constructive. Why don't you wipe the counters or stock the milk cooler or something?"

"Fine." She stood up and sulked as she walked around the diner's counter.

"I'll be right back." I flipped a bar rag over one shoulder and went outside to find Holly sitting near the front door, facing the gas pumps. Three pumps had cars at them, and an old beat-up RV was just pulling in.

"How's business?" I asked her hopefully.

"Slow," she said. "I've only had two customers. My first

one was a woman who wanted to know if her boyfriend was ever going to propose. Of course she was annoyed with me when I told her he wasn't, so no tip for me." She rolled her eyes. Then, picking lint off her shirt, she added, "I was nice anyway and told her she needed a new boyfriend and that she could go inside and talk to Sweets for a love consultation. The other customer was a ginormous truck driver who asked me to read his mind. How was *I* supposed to know what he was thinking? I'm *clairvoyant*, not a mind reader. When I told him that he was thinking about lunch, he told me that was obvious and demanded his twenty bucks back." Holly slumped down in her seat. "We're never going to make enough money like this."

"You just need more customers." As I said the words, two people who'd just finished pumping gas walked past Holly and into the store. "You've got plenty of traffic."

"I know. They go in, but they don't stop."

"You have to try harder. Be flirty. You know how to do that."

"Mercy, this is not the same as flirting with a boy. Have you ever seen those Girl Scouts trying to sell cookies in front of the grocery store?"

"Yeah. Why?"

"Well, whenever I see those girls, I avoid eye contact at all costs." She frowned. "I mean, I can't eat Girl Scout cookies and keep a figure like this. But I feel bad saying no, so I pretend to be busy so they won't talk to me."

I chuckled. "Okay?"

"Well, that's what *everyone* is doing to me. They pretend to be busy on their phones so they don't have to talk to me or look at me. They don't even want to know what I'm selling."

I rolled my eyes. "Then you're doing it wrong. Loosen

up a few buttons, Holl. *Make* them see you. Shoot, you'd think those truck drivers would give you twenty bucks just to stare at you for a few minutes."

That made her giggle. She straightened her spine and sat up taller. "I never thought about it like that." She smiled broadly. "You're right! They *should* want to pay twenty dollars to stare at this. The psychic stuff is just a bonus. I can do this."

"Good, because we're counting on you. Things aren't going so well in there. Business is dead."

"No worries. I'm going to get us our money."

Grinning excitedly, I stood back to watch her work.

With a new and improved attitude, Holly adjusted the buttons on her shirt, so that her cleavage was front and center. She adjusted her long blond waves, and then she leaned over her table and used her biceps to smash her boobs together.

Leaning against the brick wall behind her, I looked down at my own boobs. I was pretty sure that they wouldn't smash together even if I used an entire roll of duct tape. Regardless, for once, I was happy that Holly had a body that might entice men to give her money. It was the only way we were ever going to make it out of this truck stop.

It didn't take long for the next person pumping gas to finish. Soon the old man that had driven the RV into the station was hobbling towards the building with a bit of a limp like his knees might buckle at any given moment. He was a small, wrinkly man with a clean-shaven face. The question of whether or not he had any hair on top of his head was hidden beneath a flat brown tweed golf cap, which matched his brown tweed pants and his short-sleeved beige button-down shirt.

"Showtime," I heard Holly mumble under her breath. The next thing I knew, she'd turned on the Holly charm. "Well, hello there, sugar. How are you today?"

The old man stopped walking and looked over at Holly. His eyes grew to the size of silver dollars as he realized she was talking to him. He hobbled closer to her. "Why, I'm fine. How are you, my dear?"

"I'm perfect. Isn't it a beautiful day?"

The man grinned from ear to ear. "Very beautiful."

Holly stood up and walked around her table so she could talk to the man face-to-face. "Say, I'm doing fortune tellings today. Would you like to have your fortune read?"

"Fortune-telling?" he repeated as if the words weren't making sense in his head. I was pretty sure he was more concerned with Holly's proximity than he was with what she had to say.

"Yes, sir." She put her hand on his back and ushered him over to her table. She gestured for him to sit down on her extra chair. "Sit, sit."

His eyes were still wide as he obligingly sat down next to her.

"Now, it's really not hard at all. All you have to do is hold my hand."

"Hold your hand?" The old man swallowed hard and then licked his bottom lip.

"That's all. What do you say? It's only twenty dollars. Are you up for it?" Holly gave him her most winning smile.

Without even hesitating, the man reached around to his back pocket and pulled out his wallet. He plucked a twenty-dollar bill from it and handed it to Holly.

She glanced over at me and we exchanged excited smiles. Finally, I had the feeling that this might just work after all.

CHAPTER 14

An hour later, after Alba had finished unloading her truck, she reappeared in the diner. "Well, that was the easiest fifty bucks I've ever made," she said, holding up a crisp fifty.

"Jax and I have *maybe* made fifty combined in tips," I said, sitting down at the diner counter with her. It felt good to sit down. I'd been running around all morning, and because I'd slept horribly, my legs were tired, my feet were killing me, and all I wanted to do was take a nap.

Alba lowered her brows. "Rick's gonna pay you each a wage though too, right?"

"Yeah, Sweets gets ten and a quarter an hour since she doesn't get tips, so she'll make like eighty bucks or something if he lets her work all day. Jax and I only get like four an hour though."

"Doesn't he have to at least pay you minimum wage if you didn't make enough tips?"

I shrugged. "Maybe. But it's not exactly like we're *real* employees. But let's say he does. That means each of us will make eighty. That's two forty for all three. You made fifty, so that's two ninety, let's just round up to three hundred. We need Holly to bring in like another four hundred bucks."

Alba let her head fall into her hands. "Ugh, this sucks."

"Yeah," I said, nodding.

"I can't believe our fate rests in Cosmo's hands."

The radio, which had been playing a top forty ballad rock song, changed to an edgier rock song.

Alba rubbed her skull. "Ugh, how can you listen to that? Doesn't it give you a headache?"

I grinned at her. The radio station had been my choice. "No."

Forcing herself to ignore it, she shook her head. "Well, have you checked on her at all? She making any money out there?"

"Last I checked, she'd made forty. But we redid her business plan, so maybe things have picked up for her." I smiled.

"Redid her business plan? What's that mean?"

I giggled. "Trust me. You don't wanna know."

Alba pointed over my shoulder. "Hey, speak of the devil."

I swiveled around on my barstool to see Holly running towards us, a huge smile on her face.

"Girls! Oh my gosh, business has totally picked up. Mercy, you had the *best* advice."

"Ha! I knew it."

"What advice did ya give her, Red?"

I waved a hand at Alba. "Never mind that. How much have you made?"

"Since you left, I've done three more readings. So I'm up to a hundred bucks already."

"All we need is another three hundred bucks, then,"

said Alba. She winced. "There's no way. You've been out there since nine and you've only made a hundred." She glanced up at the clock on the wall. "It's almost one. There's no way you're making another three hundred in the next four hours."

"You never know," sang Holly, a wide smile on her face.

"Well, what're you doing in here? Time's ticking," said Alba.

"I came in to get something to eat. I'm *starving*. Reading fortunes and being hot takes so much out of me. I needed a little break."

"Oh, yeah," I said, nodding. "I'm sorry. I should've thought of that." I stood up, walked around the counter, and looked through the little order window at Sweets. "Hey, Sweets. Will you make Holly a sandwich?"

"What kind does she want?"

"Hey, Holl, what do you want?"

She shrugged. "Just give me a club sandwich, light on the mayo."

I looked at Sweets. "You hear that?"

She nodded back at me. "Yeah, I'll have it right out."

"Hey, Holly, how's business?" asked Jax, joining us with a pot of coffee in her hand.

"Pretty good. How about in here?"

I looked out across the room. There was a smattering of truck drivers. A married couple and their two kids who were traveling out east on a family vacation. Two high school girls giggled in a corner booth. And the little old man who'd driven up in the RV sat quietly nursing a cup of coffee at a table near the back.

Jax shrugged. "It's picked up a little, but it's nowhere near as busy as the B&B."

Sweets came out of the kitchen carrying a basket of

french fries and put it down in front of Holly. "I'm toasting your bread. Your sandwich will be out in a minute."

"Thanks, Sweets," said Holly, plucking a fry out of the basket and putting it in her mouth.

"Alba, you want something to eat?"

"Yeah, I'd take a sandwich too. Whatever's easy," said Alba. "Thanks, Sweets."

"No problem." But before Sweets could walk around the counter, the radio made a sudden sharp beeping noise. It had made the noise a couple of other times throughout the morning, but I'd been waiting on customers and hadn't had a chance to hear what it had said.

"This is a local news alert. The Baltimore Police Department has issued this alert to everyone in our listening area. Please be advised that the Baltimore Area Truck Stop Killer has struck again, killing a young married couple at a truck stop along Interstate 83 near the Brooklandville area. The killer, leaving two-dollar bills at the scene of the crime as his calling card, is thought to be on a random killing spree. His body count is now up to six. The suspect walks with a limp and is described as an older white male with gray hair. The suspect was last observed wearing a white t-shirt, khaki pants, and white sneakers. He is thought to be heading north on Interstate 83 towards Pennsylvania. A ten-thousand-dollar reward has been offered for information leading to his arrest. Please do not approach the suspect. If you see him, move away and contact the nearest police station to report the sighting. Do not attempt to apprehend him. The suspect is considered armed and extremely dangerous."

The radio beeped again until it returned to the music that had been playing.

"Oh my gosh," said Jax, her eyes round. "That's super scary."

"Yeah, it is," agreed Alba. "What did I tell you girls about truck stops?"

"Who knew a psychopathic killer was on the loose, though?" I said.

Sweets' forehead was creased as she looked across the counter at Holly. "What's the matter, Holly? Are you feeling okay?"

Holly swallowed hard and looked backwards over her shoulder. Then her head bobbed slightly and she leaned forward onto the counter. "Umm, girls," she whispered. "See that old man at the table in the back?"

"The guy whose fortune you read earlier?" I glanced back at him. He'd been sitting there for over an hour. After he'd had his fortune read, he'd come inside and paid for gas, then he'd moved his RV to the side of the building and come inside for a cup of coffee. He'd only moved from his spot once, to use the restroom, and then he'd sat back down and we'd refilled his coffee cup numerous times.

She nodded. "Yeah."

As all heads turned to look at him, Holly freaked out. "Don't all look at him!" she hissed, lowering her head to the counter so he wouldn't see her.

"What about him?" asked Jax.

"Like Mercy said, I did a psychic reading on him earlier. It was really weird."

"Weird?" said Alba, curling her lip. "Like how?"

Holly shrugged. "It wasn't crystal-clear. I could feel that he was scared. He's running from someone, and he's scared that he's going to be caught. He doesn't want to go back to wherever he came from, but he doesn't know where to go next."

Jax's mouth gaped. "What?!"

My eyes widened and I suddenly remembered seeing the picture of an old man flash across the television screen earlier that morning. The man on TV had a gray, grizzly beard and wiry gray hair, but he looked an awful lot like the freshly shaven and well-groomed man I'd served coffee to for the last hour. "Oh my gosh, I saw the mugshot of the Baltimore Truck Stop Killer on the news this morning. The volume was off, so I didn't know what they were saying, but now it makes sense."

Holly sucked in her breath. "You saw his face?" She tipped her head back towards the old man. "Was it him?"

Holding my breath and trying to look casual, I looked over Holly's shoulder again and stared at the old man. His head was down. "I don't know, he's not looking right now. It might be him."

Alba pursed her lips. "Okay, get ready to have a look, Red." She flicked her finger in his direction and curled it, and his chin lifted.

I studied the man's eyes and the shape of his face. Without his beard, he looked a little different than the man I'd seen on television, which was why I hadn't made the connection when I first saw him. But I imagined him without his beard and hat.

I sucked in my breath. "Oh my gosh, girls. That's totally him. And now that I think about it, they even showed the exact same RV when they showed his picture. Isn't that what we saw him driving earlier, Holly?"

"Yes! It's totally what he was driving!"

A hand went to Sweets' mouth. She took two steps backwards towards the kitchen. "Ohhh," she moaned. "The radio announcer said if you see him to move away. Maybe we should call the police and hide out in the kitchen until they get here. I have a lot of knives in the kitchen."

"Calm down, Sweets. We're witches," said Alba. "That old man's not about to kill us. Not if I have anything to do with it." She cracked her knuckles and then wiggled her fingers in the air as if she were warming the weapons up.

My heart pounded wildly in my chest. "I can't believe that old man killed six people. I'd never have suspected him of that in a million years."

"It's always the ones you least expect," said Sweets. "That's what my momma always used to say."

Shooting wary glances in the old man's direction, Jax nibbled on her fingernails. "Girls, this is freaking me out. We need to call the police."

Holly held her hands out. Her palms flared and hovered just above the counter. "Wait. There's a ten-thousand-dollar reward for that guy. We need to talk this out before we go doing anything hasty."

Alba wagged her finger. "I can't believe I'm about to say this, but Cosmo's right. That's a lotta dough. We could use that money right now. Not only will we get the car fixed, but my share would be enough to pay rent next semester."

"And I could replace all the clothes that were stolen," said Holly.

"I could put the money towards a new car," I said. "I'm tired of my old clunker breaking down all the time."

"So, what do we do?" asked Jax. "Just call in a tip to the police?"

"Puh," spat Alba. "There's a ten-thousand-dollar reward for this guy. Do you know how many fake tips the cops are getting right now? By the time they get around to investigating every single lead, it'll be October, the old man'll be long gone, and there'll be a string of dead bodies in his wake." Alba shook her head. "No. Just calling in a tip isn't enough to guarantee us that money. We need to take it one step farther."

I looked at Alba curiously. "One step farther? What do you mean? Like tie him up or something until the cops get here?"

"You really wanna sit around here all day waiting for the cops to show up?" asked Alba.

I shrugged. "I don't know. What other options do we have?"

"I'll tell you our other option." Alba swiveled around in her barstool to look over at the man, whose head was down again as he gazed into his coffee. "We tie him up, throw him in his RV, and *drive* him to the police station ourselves."

CHAPTER 15

"Drive him to the police station ourselves? Alba, are you insane?" asked Sweets.

"Look, I know it sounds risky, but do you know how much red tape is involved in a reward? If we just call the cops and wait for them to come pick him up, we're never gonna see that money. And we don't have the time to wait. We need our car fixed today! If we drag him over there and drop him off right in front of them, we can demand to be paid immediately."

"But what if he tries to kill *us* before we can get him to the police station?" asked Sweets. "The alert specifically said not to try and apprehend him."

"That's for normal people, not us. We're witches. He's not gonna try and kill us. We'll tie him up. We've got magic. We'll be fine." She looked at me then. "Well, what do you think, Red?"

While I liked the idea of getting the reward money and putting a serial killer behind bars, the thought of having to transport a serial killer to jail sounded a little sketchy to me.

I just wasn't sure if we had any other options. I shrugged. "I mean, I guess we could do that. What do you think, Jax?"

Jax's head bobbed as if she didn't even have to give it a second thought. "I think we're witches, and returning him is the witchly thing to do. How about you, Holly? What do you think?"

Holly swished her lips to the side as she considered Alba's proposal. "I think I want my dad's credit card back."

Alba rolled her eyes. "Try and keep up, Cosmo. We're talking about taking a killer into the police station and getting the reward money." She said the last sentence patronizingly slow, patting her hands together in front of Holly's face for effect.

"I *know* what we're talking about. But you said we'd take his RV into town. That gives us a vehicle. The only reason you wouldn't let me try and find the people that stole my dad's credit card was because we didn't have a vehicle. Well, if we take the old man in and use his RV, we could also go after the thieves."

"You can't be serious. You think we have time for that?"

Holly's head bobbed. "It's the only way I'm agreeing to this ridiculous plan of yours."

Alba shrugged her shoulders. "Whatever, Cosmo. We don't need you to agree to my plan. We'll run him in without you."

Holly looked at all of us pleadingly. "Oh, come on, girls. You have to help me get the credit card back. My dad will literally kill me if I don't."

Jax linked arms with Holly. "I think we should help Holly. Her dad's the one who offered to pay for the trip. We can't just turn our back on him now."

Sweets nodded. "Jax is right. If we're going to go to all the trouble to take the serial killer into the police station, I

ROAD TRIPPIN' WITH MY WITCHES

think we might as well see if we can't track down the thief too."

I shrugged. "If Jax and Sweets are in, I'm in too."

Alba's head dipped forward into her hand. "Ugh."

Holly clapped her hands together excitedly. "Ohhh, thank you, girls! Thank you, thank you, thank you!"

"Okay, so now we need a plan. How are we going to get that old man to go with us to the police station?" I asked.

"Obviously we'll have to tie him up," said Sweets.

"Right, but are we just supposed to walk over there and throw a rope around his shoulders and expect him to not throw a fuss? There are other customers in here!"

Sweets deflated slightly. "True."

Holly sat up brightly then. "Oh! I have an idea. What if I went back over there and told him that I had another vision about him?"

Jax furrowed her brow. "What do you mean?"

Holly shrugged. "Well, obviously he's running from the law and scared to get caught. I could go over there and tell him that I just had another vision about someone coming after him and that he better leave now."

Alba nodded. "And then the four of us could be waiting outside in his RV."

"And we tie him up when he gets in!" said Jax.

Holly nodded. "Exactly."

"Well, that should be easy enough," I said.

"But before we do that, we need to find out who stole our stuff. We didn't have a reason before to go look at the security tapes, but we do now," said Holly.

Alba sighed. "Fine. Cosmo, Shorty, and Sweets, you three keep our serial killer occupied and in the building. Red and I'll go see if we can't convince the manager to let us see the security footage from last night."

101

Holly put her hands on her hips. "No way! I should be the one watching the security footage. It was *my* stuff that was stolen."

"Nah, you need to let the old guy see you so it's not weird when you tell him you had a new vision about him. Maybe you should sit somewhere he can see you while you eat your lunch."

Holly quirked a brow. "Somewhere he can see me? So like right here?"

"Whatever. Come on, Red."

"I don't know about this, Alba," said Sweets. "I don't want to be left here alone with a serial killer."

"You're not alone, Sweets. You've got these two."

"No offense to Holly or Jax, but I don't exactly feel like they're gonna save me if a serial killer comes after me."

Jax nodded, wide-eyed. "Yeah, like what am *I* gonna do? I can't even get my magic to work yet!"

"Guys. Look at him. The guy's like ninety-five pounds soaking wet. Are you telling me you can't take an old man?"

"Maybe if he were a normal old man, but he's not. Somehow he managed to kill six people. I think he's got some major ninja skills that aren't apparent to the eye," said Jax.

Alba closed her eyes and groaned. "Oh my gosh, do I have to do *everything* around here?"

I sighed. "Look, Alba. The girls are probably right. You've got the strongest magic of the group. He doesn't look like much, but he could have a gun or a knife on him, and you're the only one that could potentially stop him. So why don't *you* stay here with Jax and Sweets? Holly and I'll go look at the security tapes. Okay?"

"They're not just gonna let you back there. They trust me. I worked for 'em all morning."

"Fine. Go get permission for us, and then Holly and I will look at the tapes and you can stay here and babysit the serial killer. Okay?"

Alba rolled her eyes but turned around and strode towards the convenience store, throwing her arms up as she walked away. "Whatever."

I knew she wanted to be a part of solving the mystery, but safety was first. "Thanks, Alba," I hollered after her.

CHAPTER 16

Ten minutes later, Holly and I sat in the small office in the back of the building, staring at their computer screen. Dallas had spent five minutes giving us a quick tutorial on how to search the security software on the computer, and now we were finally alone and ready to start searching. Each camera in the building had its own video footage. We just had to select which camera angle we thought would best show what we wanted to see.

Holly pointed to one of the monitors. "Look, that one's right over the TV screen in the diner. Let's watch that one first."

I clicked on the monitor and then slid the little time indicator backwards until it showed the group of us coming back inside after we realized the car wouldn't start.

"There we are!" said Holly, pointing at the screen.

I nodded and played the footage back, watching as we spread out and got comfortable. The two truckers we'd seen were there, quietly eating their pancakes. The three punk-rocker-looking guys were still there, flicking their little paper footballs. And the video showed Rick checking on us. I glanced over at Holly. "Okay, I'm gonna increase the speed, so it goes through the tape faster. If you see anything I don't, holler and I'll slow it down."

Holly nodded, and together we watched as we fell asleep one by one. Then we watched the two truckers get up and pay their bill before leaving. It took a while, but eventually, the table of spiky-haired guys got up and did the same. When the place was empty, except for us girls, we watched Rick go back into the kitchen. No sooner had Rick disappeared from the screen than we saw the three spiky-haired punks reenter the diner and quietly head in our direction.

Holly pointed at the screen, nodding her head. "I knew it was gonna be them. I just knew it!"

I bit my lip, waiting to see the inevitable. I'd wondered if it wasn't going to be them too. Sure enough, they all snuck over to our area. One of the guys reached inside Holly's backpack, lying on the seat, and stole her purse right out from inside. On the other side of the booth, Holly didn't even flinch. Another one of the guys took Sweets' wallet from inside her purse. A third guy poked around me, Alba and Jax but, not finding anything of interest, took off seconds later, no doubt scared that Rick would come back out and bust them or that one of us would wake up.

Shaking my head, I paused the video. "So it was them. Punks."

Holly frowned. "I can't believe they stole from us. That's so mean! Who does that?!"

"Apparently they do. Should we switch to an outdoor camera and double-check what I'm sure we already know?"

"Which is what?"

"Duh? That they stole the stuff off the top of our car too."

Holly made a circle with her mouth and nodded.

I switched cameras and rewound the footage to only seconds after they'd stolen Holly and Sweets' wallets. Sure enough, we watched as they drove their beat-up black van with the bumper stickers over to our vehicle. The sliding side door and the passenger door opened, and two guys got out. Both of them pulled out pocket knives, slicing the tie-downs that Reign had used to secure our bags to the roof. In seconds, they'd removed all the bags from the top of our car and tossed them into the back of their van. Then they loaded themselves up and took off like shots. I rewound the video and fiddled with the zoom function until I got close enough to the license plate that I could read the letters and numbers and quickly jotted them down on a piece of scratch paper on Dallas's desk.

"I'm just gonna switch camera angles here and see if we can't find out which direction they went after they left the truck stop."

Holly nodded. "Ooh, yeah, that's a good idea."

I went back to the main screen and selected the camera angle that faced the road. Adjusting the time, we were able to see that the van took a right towards the I-83 South ramp before disappearing off the surveillance video. It looked like they were headed into Baltimore. I threw my hands up. "Well. There it is. We know who stole all of our stuff. We know what they're driving. And we know their license plate number. I think we figured out everything we needed to know."

Holly stood up. "Let's get back to the girls, then. We've got a lot of work to do."

~

BACK IN THE DINER, Alba jumped us the minute we reappeared. "Well? What did you find out?"

"It was those kids," said Holly, her face contorted into an angry pout. "I knew it was going to be."

Alba groaned. "Ugh, I wondered. There weren't a lot of people around here at that time."

"Do you remember seeing that black junker van parked out front when we got here? It had bumper stickers all over it."

"Mmm, I vaguely remember it."

"Well, that was theirs. They also stole the stuff from on top of our car. I got their plates."

"You got their plates? That's awesome. We can just give that information to the cops and let them handle it," said Alba, grinning from ear to ear.

But Holly wasn't having it. She swiped her hands in the air. "Oh, no. We're getting my stuff back *today*. They took a right, heading towards Baltimore. We'll figure out a way to track them down."

"How? Whatcha gonna do? Knock on every business's door between here and Baltimore and ask to see their security footage of the road?"

Holly put a hand on either hip and stood up tall. "Maybe."

"Ohhhh, no. No. Absolutely not. That kinda crap'll take all day. We have places to be and people to deliver to the cops. That's our priority."

Holly snapped a finger in the air at Alba. "You're not the boss of this operation, Alba. So step off."

"Step off?!" bellowed Alba, taking a step towards Holly.

I pushed my way between the two of them. "Okay, okay.

Oh my gosh. You two definitely need a summer apart. Listen, Holly. It's not feasible to stop at every business along the interstate to watch their security footage. We're going in that direction anyway since the police are that way. Maybe we'll get lucky and see their van. Who knows?"

Staring over my shoulder, Holly's eyes suddenly grew wide. "Hold the phone," she said breathlessly. She rushed towards the table where the three young guys had been sitting that morning.

I stared at her curiously, tipping my head sideways, wondering what in the world she was doing as she squatted down low and picked something up off the floor.

Turning around, she held up what she'd found. It was one of their little paper footballs. "Look!" she said.

Before I could even respond, Holly's eyes went blank and her knees started to buckle. "Oh, crap. Alba, get her a chair. She's having a vision."

Alba was way ahead of me. Before I could even get all the words out, Alba had flicked a finger, and the chair from the table beside Holly spun around and caught her as she started going down. She landed in it with a plop.

I raced to her side to keep her from flopping sideways. "Holly!"

And then suddenly Jax was beside us. "What happened to her?"

"She picked that napkin up off the floor. I think she's having a vision," I explained.

And then suddenly, the serial killer was behind us, staring over our shoulders at Holly. "Is she alright?" he asked.

Feeling his presence behind me made my adrenaline pump faster. "Oh. Yeah, she's fine."

"Thanks, though," chirped Jax, trying to act natural,

though I could tell by her wide eyes that she was feeling just as uneasy as I was to have a serial killer standing in such close proximity to us.

But the man didn't move. Apparently he wasn't ready to sit back down again, even though I was willing him to. "What happened to her? It looked like she fainted."

"This happens to her sometimes," explained Jax.

I shot her the stink-eye to shut her up. We didn't need to explain anything to this guy.

Jax shrank back. "Yeah, okay."

"Hey, uh, Shorty, why don't you and Sweets see if you can't wake Rick up? It's probably about time we get out of here, don't you think?"

"Get out of here?" Jax's forehead crinkled up as she looked at Alba curiously.

"Yeah, you know. We have all those plans for later today," said Alba. "I'll help Red take care of Cosmo."

Jax's eyes widened as she realized what Alba was talking about. "Oohhh, our *plans*. Umm, yeah. I'll go tell Rick we have to go." She smiled uncomfortably at the old man before turning and walking away.

The old man looked up at Alba. "Why does this happen to her? Does she have a health condition? Is she diabetic? Has she eaten anything today?"

"She started to eat her sandwich," I explained. "And then we got sidetracked. Really, it's no big deal."

"She's psychic," he said, as if he was telling us something we didn't already know. "She did a reading for me earlier."

"Did she?" I smiled uncomfortably.

Alba nodded then. "Yeah, she passes out like this when she has a new vision. I'll bet that's what was happening.

She probably saw you sitting over there and had another vision about you."

His eyes widened. "You think so?"

Alba's head bobbed up and down earnestly. "For sure."

"Do you think she'd tell me if she saw anything, umm, important happening in my future?" he asked, shifting his weight awkwardly.

"When she snaps outta this, I could tell her you'd like to know," suggested Alba.

The man's head bobbed up and down. "Oh, yeah. I definitely want to know."

"Okay, then you go on and sit back down. We'll try and get her to snap out of her vision, and we'll send her over when she's feeling strong enough. Okay?"

The man nodded at Alba and then turned and walked away. I was thankful that Alba was able to be stern with him and convince him to leave, because he was creeping me out standing so close. "Good job, Alba," I whispered. "Good thinking."

"Right? That worked out perfectly. Now he's totally gonna buy it when she says she had a new vision about the cops coming after him." She looked down at Holly, whose lashes were starting to flutter. "Look, she's starting to come out of it. We're gonna need to work quickly. I'm gonna go get the girls. We'll be outside in the guy's camper. When Holly's ready, you need to have her do what we talked about. The second she does that, he'll take off and get in his RV where we'll be waiting for him."

"Alba, I'm worried. What if he gets the better of us?"

"That's why you and Holly aren't with us. If something happens and things go haywire, then you'll be standing by to call the cops. I'll text you a picture of his plates, alright?"

I nodded.

"Okay, I'm outta here."

"Hey, Alba, be safe, okay? This isn't a game."

"I know, Red. You be safe too."

The second Alba took off to round up Sweets and Jax, I looked down at Holly. She was moaning softly now. I knelt down in front of her and shook her shoulders. "Holly, it's okay. You're having a vision. Can you hear me?"

"Huh?" she moaned, as her lids fluttered open. "Mercy?"

"Hey, Holl. Yeah, it's me. You alright?"

A hand went to her forehead then. "Oh, yeah. I had a vision. I saw those guys who stole our stuff."

"I figured. You picked up one of those little folded pieces of paper they were playing with and then immediately went out like a light. What'd you see?"

"They're in a park somewhere," she said, rubbing her temples. "I couldn't tell where, though."

"Did you see anything else?"

"There were a lot of people around. And there was a stage set up. Like they're at an event of some sort."

"Okay, well, that's something. There can't be that many big events around. We'll figure it out. But we have to get going. Alba's taking the girls out to the RV. While you were out, our serial killer came to check on you. He saw you pass out."

Holly's eyes widened. "He did?"

"Yeah. He knows you were having another vision, and Alba told him it might be about him."

Holly sat up a little straighter. "You're kidding."

"Not kidding. But this is good. Now he's going to be receptive to whatever you have to say. It'll be more believable this way."

Holly nodded. "Okay, well, gimme a minute. I'm still a little woozy. I never did finish my lunch."

"You want some orange juice or something?"

"Yeah, orange juice would be great. And maybe a slice of that pie on the counter?"

I smiled at her. "Orange juice and pie, coming up."

CHAPTER 17

W hen her plate was empty and her juice was gone,
Holly stood up. Alba, Jax, and Sweets had already
left the building almost five minutes prior, and I'd seen
Rick's head bobbing around in the kitchen, so I knew we
were all safe to leave. Holly and I had gone over what she
was going to say a handful of times, which seemed to calm
her nerves slightly, but she'd still insisted on me going with
her. Not that I blamed her, I wouldn't have wanted to talk
to a serial killer all by myself either. So, arm in arm, we
shuffled over to the killer's table.

The old man still sat there, looking down at his coffee,
lost in thought.

"Sir?" Holly's voice trembled as she spoke.

He looked up at her anxiously. "Are you feeling better?"

Holly nodded and gave him a tight smile. "Much better.
Thanks."

"Your friends said that happens to you sometimes when
you have a psychic vision. Is that what was happening?"
He looked anxious to hear what she had to say.

"Yes. I saw you sitting over here, and I guess it made me have a vision."

His eyes widened. "About me?"

Holly nodded. "I thought it was only right that I come over here and warn you about it."

The man swallowed hard. "Warn me?"

She nodded. "There are a lot of people after you."

His face went white. "Do they know where I am?"

"They do. They're on their way here now."

"Now?"

"Yes. If my vision is accurate, they should be here soon. You're not safe here."

The man scooted off his chair and stood up. "I didn't think they'd be able to find me this quickly."

"Someone must have seen you," she said ominously. "You better go. Otherwise it might be too late."

The old man plucked a couple of bills from his wallet and put them on the counter. Then he met Holly's eyes. "Thank you."

With her lips pressed together in a thin line, she nodded but didn't answer.

Without another word, the old man shuffled towards the diner's side entrance. As he moved, I was once again reminded that he walked with a bit of a limp, confirming even more solidly that this was indeed the man the police were looking for.

Knowing full well that we were sending the man into a trap, my pulse raced wildly as he left the building.

Holly and I raced over to the counter. "Hey, Rick, we're leaving," I hollered.

"You're coming back later, right? For your paychecks?" he shouted back, looking at us through the opening to the kitchen.

"Yeah, for sure. We just have to go take care of a little business."

"Okay, no problem. I feel so much better after that nap. I owe you girls."

Holly and I waved at him before taking off out the front door and sneaking around to the side of the building. Standing with our backs up against the wall, Holly and I peered around the corner of the truck stop. The old man's RV, parked on the east side of the building next to Phil's repair shop, sat quietly in its parking spot. Onlookers never would've guessed that not only was the RV driven by a homicidal maniac, but that five witches were about to abduct said homicidal maniac.

I stared at the windows, trying to catch a glimpse of anything inside, but there was nothing. I wondered if the old man had even gone inside. Had he somehow escaped? Or had he never made it to the RV in the first place? Perhaps Holly's warning had scared him so badly that he'd decided to ditch his vehicle and take off on foot. Though that option seemed unlikely as he wasn't a very fast mover and wouldn't get very far on foot.

"What's taking them so long?" hissed Holly. "You think they're okay?"

"I don't know. Let's give them another minute."

She nodded and we stared at the RV, waiting for anything to happen. And then all of a sudden, the truck started moving wildly, rocking from side to side. "Mercy!" breathed Holly. "Should we go help?"

"No. Alba said not to move until she gives us the signal. We don't want to get in their way."

That was when the RV stopped rocking and a figure appeared in the window. It was Alba, sliding into the driver's seat. She gave two beeps of the horn. It was the signal we'd been waiting for.

"There it is, Holl. Come on."

Feeling like a criminal myself, I ducked low and led the way to the RV with Holly hot on my heels. Before we'd even gotten to the door, it flew open and Jax beckoned us in. "Hurry, hurry, get in!"

Hearing the horn blast, the mechanic stuck his head out of his shop. When he saw Holly climb inside the vehicle, he pointed at me. "Hey! I've got your car parts. I should have it done by five."

I winced but stopped in my tracks and looked back at Phil. He'd seen us getting into the RV. This was bad. I forced a smile on my face. "Great. Don't worry. We'll be back!"

"Well, I close at seven, so if you're not back by then, you won't get your car until Tuesday. I'm closed on Sundays, and Monday is a holiday."

"Mercy! Come on!" hissed Jax as I heard the RV roar to life.

My heart raced. "Oh, don't worry. We'll be back long before that. Gotta go!"

Phil bobbed his head and then dropped it to look at the part he held in his hand before going back into the garage. He didn't seem to care that we were taking off in an RV that wasn't ours.

The second he was out of sight, I jumped in the vehicle and Alba took off before I even had a chance to shut the door, but the force of the takeoff slammed the door shut for me. "Geez, Alba!"

"We gotta get outta here before someone realizes what's going on," she said, hitting the gas. The RV hit a pair of speed bumps, making the whole thing rock from side to side as each tire went over each bump in turn. Right before leaving the parking lot, she hit the gas again, and as she took a right towards the interstate, the RV seemed to rock sideways onto two wheels, squealing around the turn.

"Alba! You're gonna kill us!" I hollered.

"Sorry, this thing drives weird," she said.

Finally back on all four wheels and on a smooth surface, I had a chance to catch my breath and look around. The inside of the RV was quaint and just as vintage as the outside. Up high, above the driver's seat and the passenger's seat was a full-size bed. Directly across from the door, Sweets and Jax sat on a tan-and-rust-colored plaid sofa, and just to the left of the door were two rust-colored swiveling captain's chairs and a small fold-down table. Further to the left and towards the back of the vehicle was a kitchen, with old-style wood counters and cabinetry and a stainless-steel sink, and further yet, there was another room at the tail end of the camper with the door closed.

I frowned. "Where is he?"

"In the bathroom," said Sweets, pointing towards the closed door.

Jax's head bobbed animatedly, her eyes bright with excitement. "We tied him up. You wanna see?"

I felt like I needed to. I needed to make sure that he was safely secured before I'd be able to relax. "Sure."

Dropping Emily onto the seat beside her, Jax leapt off the sofa and beckoned for me to follow her. When we got to the door, she held a finger up to her lips. "Shhh."

I nodded and she put her hand on the doorknob and then threw it open. Sure enough, there he was. The old man. They'd duct-taped his mouth closed and wrapped more tape around his body, trapping his arms down by his side. He sat with his knees drawn up to his chest in the small bathtub, his ankles taped too. The second he saw me and Holly, his eyes grew huge and he started making noises in the back of his throat.

Holly's own eyes mirrored the man's, and she backed towards the living room, out of his view.

I followed her. Seeing him like that didn't make me feel much better. Instead I felt slightly nauseous. I frowned. "Close it, Jax."

Jax slammed the door shut and the group of us went back to the RV's small living room. I took a seat across the little folding table from Holly while Jax resumed her cross-legged position on the sofa next to Sweets.

I shook my head, in awe of what we'd just managed to pull off. "Oh my gosh. I can't believe we seriously just caught a serial killer."

"Me either," agreed Sweets. "My heart just about beat out of my chest!"

Smiling broadly, Jax squeezed Emily to her chest. "Ohhh, me too, me too!"

Even Alba got in on the excitement. She fist-pumped the air with her free hand. "Woohoo! We did it!"

"This is amazing, girls," breathed Holly. "We're so close to that ten-thousand-dollar reward that I can almost taste it!"

"Oh man, Tony's gonna be jazzed when I tell him I've got rent covered for next semester," said Alba from the front seat, grinning from ear to ear.

Hearing the girls so excited made me feel a little better. We'd done a noble thing, taking a dangerous serial killer off the streets. I couldn't wait to tell Mom, Reign, and Hugh what we'd done. I settled back in my seat, smiling, thinking about how I might spend my share of the reward money.

We'd been sitting there for only a few long seconds

when Holly looked over at me with a wrinkled nose. "Guys, is it just me or does it smell *really* bad in here?"

"It definitely smells damp," said Sweets, nodding in agreement.

Jax's head bobbed up and down, and I noticed for the first time that her eyes were all watery and red. "Yeah, and it's making my allergies horrible," she said with a sniffle.

I frowned. "Maybe there's mold in here."

"Ugh, I think I'm allergic to mold," said Jax, fighting back a sneeze.

"Well, at least we won't have to be in here long. Just until we handle our business," I said, giving Jax a tight smile that said *hang in there.*

"So now what?" asked Sweets, looking around.

"Now, we need to figure out where those thieves are. They're headed to Baltimore. I had a vision about them," said Holly.

Jax wiggled her nose again to keep from sneezing. "What did you see?"

"Well, for starters, it was those punk rocker guys that stole our stuff."

Sweets nodded. "That's what Alba said. I can't say I'm surprised."

"Yeah, we weren't either," I agreed.

"I saw them at a park. There was a stage behind them, and a whole bunch of other people were there milling around. Like they were at some kind of big event."

"Oh, maybe we could—"

Suddenly there was a pounding on the bathroom wall.

I froze. My eyes were wide as I stared at the girls. It was the killer.

Everyone else froze too. Only Jax moved as she did her best to sniffle without making any noise.

And then the pounding sounded again.

Jax lifted her chin in my direction, her silent commanding gesture telling me to go check on him.

I widened my eyes and shook my head.

She nodded back at me.

I rolled my eyes. Alba was driving. There was no way Sweets, Jax, or Holly was going to check on him. They were too chicken. I was going to have to be the brave one. I sucked up my breath and walked to the bathroom door. My heart pulsed in my chest. Hesitantly, I put my hand on the doorknob and exhaled. *You got this, Mercy.*

I slowly pressed down the handle, and all of a sudden, the door flew open.

CHAPTER 18

Catching me off guard, the door hit me and I stumbled backwards against the wall. Though his arms were still tied down by his sides and his ankles were wrapped, the man was on his feet. He hopped forward and head-butted me in the face before I had a chance to catch my balance.

Instantly, I felt pressure followed by pain. My eyes almost immediately watered and blood spurted from my nose. "Ahhh!" I screamed. "He head-butted me!"

With me distracted, the man hopped past me and towards the living room, where Jax, Holly, and Sweets all sat staring at him incredulously.

"Alba!" screamed Jax, her legs pulled up close to her chest. "He's loose!"

Alba glanced up in her rearview mirror, but since she was still driving, she was unable to help. "Red, do something!"

"A little busy here," I hollered as I searched the kitchen for a towel to stop the blood from gushing out of my nose.

"Mercy!" cried Jax, staring at the man as if he were a spider crawling towards her. "Help!"

Sweets and Holly simply stared at him too, apparently unsure of what to do to stop him.

The old man hopped past them all, trying to get to the door.

Still gushing blood from my nose, I lifted an arm without even thinking and fired a bolt of electrical energy from my hand just as Alba swerved the RV, trying to knock him off his feet. My electrical burst missed him and hit the passenger seat instead, immediately igniting it.

"Fire!" cried Holly, pointing to the seat.

Crap.

The man turned to look at me, his eyes wide. I could tell he was freaking out now. And if I were being honest, I'd have to admit I was a little freaked out too. I'd never fired an electrical burst of energy before. Yes, I'd levitated things, but I'd never tried to shoot anything with energy before. So to find out I had that ability both shocked and impressed me.

But I'd revealed my powers to the old man, and if he was scared before, now he was really afraid. He struggled to get to his feet again, but it was futile. Not only was he in an awkward position with his arms bound by his side and his ankles wrapped, but there was also no way he was getting back up while the vehicle was moving, not with Alba swerving like crazy.

Finally finding a towel in one of the kitchen drawers, I held it to my nose and tilted my head back. My shirt and my Converse sneakers were now covered in blood, as was the floor of the RV. I started towards the front of the vehicle.

"Get him, Mercy!" cheered Jax.

But I stopped short of him and instead turned towards

the door, where I grabbed the fire extinguisher off the wall, pulled the pin, and fired white foam at the burning seat, extinguishing the fire. Then I turned and looked at the old man. "Just where exactly did you think you were going?"

The man cowered on the floor. I flicked my finger at him, magically lifting him off the floor.

"Ahh, ahhh, aaaahhhhhh!" His screams were muffled by the tape on his mouth as I moved him over to my seat and gently sat him down.

I walked over to stand in front of him. His eyes were wild as I reached down and ripped the tape from his face. This time when he screamed, his cries were louder and more clear.

"Ahhhhhh!"

"Mercy, what are you doing?!" hissed Sweets. "Why are you taking that off?"

"Because he can hardly breathe like that," I said. My own voice was muffled by the cotton towel I held on my nose.

"So?! He's a serial killer. Who cares if he can't breathe!" snapped Holly.

The man stopped screaming. His head jerked over to look at Holly. "What did you just say?"

Holly's eyes widened and her lips pressed together, zipping her lips shut and refusing to speak again.

When she wouldn't talk, he looked over at me. "What did she just say?"

"She said you're a serial killer, who cares if you can't breathe." I shrugged. I really didn't care if he could breathe either. He'd killed all those poor innocent people, and he'd head-butted me and ruined my favorite sneakers. In that moment, I agreed that he didn't deserve to breathe. But I was also pretty sure we weren't going to get the reward money if we turned a dead guy into the cops.

"Serial killer?!" he cried, his forehead crinkled up. "I'm not a serial killer."

I leaned my head back and pinched the bridge of my nose, trying to get the bleeding to stop. "Oh, come on. We're not stupid. I saw your picture on the news. It was you. I'm sure of it."

"Y-you saw my picture on the news?" He looked like a deer caught in the headlights.

"Yup. Several times," I said.

Sweets nodded. "The jig is up. Once we heard the description of the Baltimore Area Truck Stop Killer, and we saw your picture, and Holly did her reading on you and discovered you were on the run, we knew it was you."

Jax sniffled and pointed at him in a sudden burst of courage. "Yeah, we know it was you!"

He shook his head. "I don't understand. Why would you girls pick up a serial killer?"

"For the money," said Holly matter-of-factly.

"Holly!" hissed Sweets. "Don't *tell* him that."

"The money? What money?" he asked, looking around at each of us, waiting for one of us to spill the beans.

Jax frowned at Sweets. "Why can't we tell him?" When Sweets couldn't think of an answer to that, Jax turned to look at the old man. "There's a ten-thousand-dollar reward for your head."

The man looked utterly frightened at the sound of that. "For my head?!"

"Well, and the rest of your body," said Jax with a giggle.

"Alive?" he asked, his face still filled with horror.

"Yes, alive," I said, sitting down across from the man between Sweets and Jax on the sofa.

"Oh, thank God," he breathed.

"And you're lucky Maryland doesn't have the death penalty anymore. Because after killing six innocent people and ruining my favorite sneakers, that's probably what you deserve."

"T-the death penalty?" he stuttered.

I nodded and pulled the rag away from my face. I was pretty sure the bleeding was letting up. "Why'd you kill all those people anyway?"

He shook his head. "Y-you don't understand. I didn't *kill* anyone."

Holly rolled her eyes. "Like we believe that?"

"No kidding," agreed Jax. "*You're* the bad guy. Like bad guys really tell the truth?"

Sweets lifted her pointer finger up into the air. "Exactly. Rule number one. Never trust a serial killer."

"But I didn't kill anyone!"

"Look, sir..." Holly looked at the old man curiously. "Wait. What's your name?"

"Henry. My name's Henry," he said frantically.

"Okay, look, Henry. There is absolutely *no doubt* in our minds that you're the one the cops are looking for. I know you're scared of being caught. I felt your fear when I did your reading earlier today. You're running from what you did. You're scared of being caught, and you know that people are chasing you. Mercy saw you and this vehicle on the news, too. We know it's you, so there's really no need to lie about it anymore." She looked down at her fingernails. "Now. Girls. Can we *please* get back to what we were talking about before we were so *rudely* interrupted?"

"What were we talking about?" asked Sweets.

"About where those thieves are!"

127

"Oh yeah." Sweets nodded. "But how are we supposed to know where that park is?"

Holly lifted her shoulder. "Maybe we could try a spell."

"What kind of spell?" I asked.

"I don't know. There's gotta be something that would work."

"We could try a locator spell," suggested Sweets with a shrug. "That's like Witchcraft 101."

Jax clapped her hands excitedly. Now that she knew she had powers, she was eager to learn to use them. "Oooh, I'm in, I'm in."

"Wait just a second here." Henry looked at each of us curiously. "Witchcraft? Is that what's going on here? You girls are witches?"

"Duh," said Holly with a giggle. "I read your mind. She picked you up with her powers and started your RV on fire with her finger." She turned to look at me then. "Speaking of which, since when can you do *that* little trick?"

I smirked and threw my hands up. "That one's new to me. I wasn't even trying. It... it just *happened*."

"Well, it was pretty cool. I'm jelly," said Jax.

"Yeah, very cool," agreed Sweets.

Holly looked back at Henry. "So if you didn't realize we were witches, how else did you think all of that stuff was happening?"

He shook his head. "I don't know. I'm old. I guess I thought I was just imagining things."

Holly quirked a brow. "Oh. Nope," she chirped. Then she held up a hand. "I mean, *yes*, you're old. But nope, you weren't imagining things."

Henry frowned. All the talk of spells, and the fact that I'd nearly zapped him and instead had lit the car seat on fire, had him properly freaked out. He pressed his lips together in a thin line and scooted back in his seat as if to say he was done talking.

I smiled at him. "Don't worry about all the witchy stuff, Henry. We have to make a pit stop before we take you into the station for our reward money."

"Sweets, I think doing a locator spell is an excellent idea," said Holly, ignoring Henry's concern over us being witches. "But how are we going to do it if we don't even know those guys' names? Without that, I don't know how it would work."

I leaned back, pulled a little piece of paper from my pocket and held it up. "We don't have their name, but we've got their license plate number. Maybe that'll work instead."

Alba looked over her shoulder and hollered back at us, "What are you guys doing back there?"

"We're gonna do a spell and see if we can't figure out where those punks are that stole our stuff," I hollered back.

"Well, there's an exit coming up. How am I supposed to know if I should get off on it?"

I waved at her. "Just keep going straight. Hopefully we'll have an address for you soon."

"Well, you better hurry. Baltimore isn't that far away."

"Yeah, I know. Hang tight." I turned back to the group and put the piece of paper down on the table. "Jax. Go see if you can find any candles in the kitchen."

Jax hopped up. "Got it."

"Holly, go check the glove compartment in the front and see if there's an atlas or a map or something."

"I'm on it."

"Sweets, we need a hanging pendulum or a necklace or something."

129

Sweets nodded. "We can use my necklace," she said and began to remove her necklace.

"Perfect. While you girls work on that stuff, I'm going to wash my hands and see if I can't get all this blood off my shoes." I shot Henry the stink-eye.

He sank further down into his seat. "Oops. My bad."

CHAPTER 19

"Mercy, I can't find any candles. Will flashlights work? I found two." Jax held up a pair of long cylindrical flashlights.

I shrugged as I adjusted the mildewy men's V-neck t-shirt I'd found in a cabinet in the bathroom. While it smelled bad, at least it didn't look like I'd just axed someone to death. "I don't know. I mean, we can try. Do they work?"

Jax tried the switches and then nodded. "Yup."

"Okay, put 'em on the table and we'll see if it does the trick."

Sweets handed me her necklace. "Here, Mercy, you can use my necklace."

"Thanks, Sweets. Any luck, Holly?" I looked up front to where Holly was now seated in the passenger's seat, rifling through the glove compartment.

"Yeah, I found an atlas. It's really old. The pages are yellow."

"That's okay. It should get us in the general area."

Holly brought the atlas back, opened it up to Maryland, and placed it on the table.

I set the flashlights up on end, putting one on the north side of the map and one on the south side. I shook my head. "Girls, we're supposed to have four candles, one at each of the cardinal directions. We've only got two and they aren't even candles. They're flashlights. I honestly don't think this is going to work."

"We have no other choice. We have to try, Merc," said Holly.

I sighed. We really didn't have anything to lose. I held Sweets' necklace up over the map, just high enough so that the gold heart attached to the thin chain didn't touch the paper. It swayed gently, and when its gentle rhythm finally came to a stop, I looked up at the girls. "Okay, here we go." I let out a breath and closed my eyes.

"Keeper of Lost and Missing Things,
Unlock the magic which this item brings.
Its rightful owner can't be found,
The time has come to look around.
Whether by the mountains, sea, or snow,
We don't know which way to go.
So take this object which once was theirs,
And on this map, show us where
We will find them, where they'll be.
Their just karma is our destiny.
So point the necklace and stop its swing,
Oh Keeper of Lost and Missing things."

The four of us chanted the spell we'd learned during one of our first weeks at the Paranormal Institute for Witches. We all watched closely as the necklace moved. It was only a slight motion, and I couldn't tell if it was doing it magically or if it was the rhythm of the car or because my hand was shaky.

"It's not working," I finally whispered.

Sweets took the necklace from my hand. "Let me try."

We repeated the chant again and again, until finally we gave up.

"It's not going to work," said Jax sadly. "Darn it! I wanted to use my powers!"

"You'll get to use your powers eventually, Jax. Don't worry. I think it was the fact that we didn't have any candles. I guess flashlights don't work."

Jax frowned and sniffled again. "No, I think it didn't work because I haven't figured out how to properly use my magic." She looked at her fingers. "It just isn't fair. Mercy, you have all kinds of cool powers. You can see ghosts. You can see through the eyes of animals. You can do telekinesis like Alba. And now you can actually zap things! Sweets is a matchmaker. Holly is a psychic and an amazing magical esthetician."

"You really think I'm amazing?" asked Holly, her eyes brightening.

"Yes! Of course I do! But it's not fair. I *finally* got my powers, but I still haven't figured out what *I'm* good at yet."

I patted Jax on the back. "Don't worry, Jax. Your powers will eventually present themselves to you. It won't be all at once. One day, you'll just go to do something and you'll realize you did it magically."

"Yeah, Jax. You know you have your powers. Now you just have to wait and see what the universe is going to give you," said Sweets with a shrug.

"Not to interrupt, but if I could just say something here?" cut in Henry. "I think what your friends are trying to say is that it's better for things in life to happen organically than to force them. Life is about patience."

Jax frowned and let out a heavy sigh. "Yeah, I know. You're right. I've just never been very good at having patience."

Holly grinned. "We know, Jax. We totally know."

"Have you guys figured out where we're goin' yet?" asked Alba. "Traffic's starting to get really heavy, and I have no idea where I'm going."

"Our spell didn't work," I hollered at her. "Can't we just drive around looking at all the parks in Baltimore?"

"You serious, Red? Do you know how many parks a city of this size probably has? It'd take us a week to drive around to all of 'em."

"Yeah, but they have to be big parks if they're having a big event," I said.

Suddenly, Holly sucked in her breath. "Oh my gosh. Duh. I never even thought about it like that before. If there's a big event going on in Baltimore this weekend, don't you think it would be all over social media or, like, on a Baltimore events calendar online somewhere?"

"Yes!" agreed Jax. "Everyone, get on your phones. See if you can't find out what events are in Baltimore this weekend."

I shook my head as I pulled my phone out of my back pocket. "Wow, I can't believe we're just now thinking of this."

"I'm on the City of Baltimore's website," said Sweets.

"I just googled 'events Memorial Day weekend Baltimore,'" said Holly. "There are a couple of things going on this weekend. There's an art and music festival in Hollins Market," she said, scanning the website. "Food trucks, outdoor sculptures and other art exhibits, and some local bands are playing on three stages."

"Here's another one," chimed in Sweets. "There's a free summer concert in Belvedere Square."

"I see that one," said Holly. "Oh, but it says it was last night."

Sweets nodded. "Yup. Sorry, I didn't see that."

Holly shook her head. "I don't think it's the Hollins Market one. The vision I saw was clearly in a big open park. There was a lot of green."

"Ooh!" squealed Jax. "Look at this one!" She held her phone up to show a big green park with people standing around in front of a stage.

Holly's eyes grew huge. "That's almost exactly what I saw in my vision, Jax. Where is that?"

"It says Druid Hill Park in Baltimore. There's a music festival going on there right now."

"Where did you find that, Jax?" asked Holly.

"Instagram."

I typed 'Druid Hill Park music festival Baltimore' into my phone's search engine. In seconds, I saw the festival that Jax had pictures of on her phone. That was when something caught my eye. "Girls. The band *The Punk Heroes of Baltimore* is playing there today."

Holly rolled her eyes. "Oh my gosh. Seriously, Mercy? Now is not the time for us to go see some obscure punk band that you're in love with."

"What are you talking about, Holly? I've never even heard of this band before today."

She shook her head. "I don't understand. Then what does that have to do with anything?"

"Those guys that stole our stuff had a Punk Heroes bumper sticker on the van they were driving."

"No way?" said Jax.

"Yeah, I noticed it when we got to the truck stop late last night."

"That's gotta be where they are, then," said Holly. "It's at the Druid Hill Park in Baltimore."

I nodded. "Now we just need to get directions."

Sweets grabbed the atlas and moved up to the front of the RV. "I'll help navigate, Alba."

"Thanks, Sweets." I handed Jax the two flashlights. "Here, Jax. You can put these wherever you found them."

She got up and stowed them in the drawer she'd found them in and then came back and plopped down on the seat next to me, hugging Emily to her chest. She sniffled. "This RV smell is making me miserable."

"We could open a window," I suggested.

"Oh, yeah, that'd be great." We turned around and worked on opening the RV's windows. When both sides were open, a nice breeze was able to flow through the camper.

Jax sat back and smiled. "Ohh, yeah. That feels good." But just as soon as she'd said it, her nose wrinkled and she sniffled again, trying to stifle another sneeze. She held a finger to her nose.

"Don't fight the sneeze, Jax. That's not good for your skin," said Holly. "It can rupture your blood vessels."

"Are you guys talking about holding back a sneeze?" asked Sweets, hollering back at us.

"Yeah, why?"

"Oh, I just read an article in *Newsweek* that said a guy ruptured his throat and died from holding back a sneeze. It's really bad for you."

"Seriously?" I hollered back.

"Yeah. It can also rupture your ears or cause a brain

aneurism, so you're really not supposed to do that. It can kill you."

"Okay, Jax. You heard Sweets. No more holding back your sneezes."

Jax's eyes widened. It was clear they were watering up badly again. "Okay, I won't," she said, and then promptly let out a sneeze all over Emily.

"Eww," squealed Holly. "I didn't say you didn't need to use a tissue."

But before an apology could come out of Jax's mouth, a weird thing happened. Emily, Jax's stuffed unicorn, suddenly began to grow. Jax held her out in front of herself with both hands. "Emily! What's happening to you?"

But the stuffed unicorn just kept growing larger and larger until Jax couldn't even handle holding her in her hands anymore. The stuffed animal dropped to its feet on the floor.

Holly scrambled to get her feet off the floor. She crouched up in her seat, her eyes nearly bugging out of her head. "What is happening right now?"

Henry's face was covered with shock, but as he was still wrapped in duct tape, the man was unable to move.

"Jax, what did you do?" I asked, staring at the unicorn that was now almost the size of a full-grown horse.

"Do?" cried Jax. "Mercy, I didn't *do* anything. I just sneezed!"

"Then how is this happening right now?"

Jax cuddled up next to me as Emily continued to grow. She peered around my arm at her stuffed animal. "I have no idea."

When Emily was the size of a full-grown horse, she stopped growing. And as we all stared at her, her pink and yellow striped tail suddenly whipped up into the air.

My mouth gaped open.

"Did you guys just see what I saw?" asked Holly.

Jax nodded. "Emily's tail just moved."

"What's happening back there?" asked Sweets, turning around again. When she saw a full-sized horse standing in the aisle between the seats, she let out a blood-curdling scream. "Ahhhh!"

"What the—" hollered Alba, looking in her rearview mirror. "How'd a horse get in here?"

"It's not a horse, Alba. It's a unicorn," cried Sweets.

"Not just any unicorn," hollered Jax. "It's Emily, and she's alive!"

CHAPTER 20

"Ahhhh!" screamed Sweets again.

Emily let out a wild whinny and shook her head, making her glittery rainbow mane sparkle in the sunlight. Just like she'd been as a stuffed animal, her body was all white, but she had a trio of pink, purple, and yellow stars on her rump. She had an iridescent gold spiral horn, and the insides of her ears were pink.

Hearing Sweets' screams seemed to make Emily nervous. She bucked about in the center aisle, throwing out her hooves behind her.

We all ducked and tried to get out of her way, except for Henry, who was tied up.

"Hellllllp!" he hollered. "Get me outta here!"

I flicked a finger at him, lifting him into the air and moving him into the kitchen, where he was a little further away from Emily's ninja kicks.

Curled up in a ball on the sofa, Jax slowly unfolded and began to creep towards Emily, holding her hands out in front of her. "Emily! It's me. It's Jax. It's okay. Don't be scared. I'm not gonna hurt you."

139

But Emily continued to bounce around the RV. One of her hind legs shot out and caught one of the RV's windows squarely, sending the aluminum frame shooting out onto the interstate and leaving a gaping hole in the wall. We all stared, frozen. Except Jax. She continued to try and approach the unicorn.

"Shhhh," cooed Jax. "Emily, it's okay." She managed to get a hand on Emily's body and slowly worked it up her frame until she was alongside her neck.

The unicorn seemed still scared, but she stopped bucking like a wild animal. Her nose flared and, shaking her head, she let out a series of puffs of air from her nose.

"Shhhh," whispered Jax. "It's okay. I'm Jax. Remember me?" She got right up to Emily's face, so they were eye to eye now. Jax patted the unicorn's head and mane and stroked her face.

"Jax! How did Emily turn into a real unicorn?!" asked Sweets, trying to restrain her fear.

"I don't know, Sweets. It—it just happened. One second she was a stuffed animal, and then all of a sudden she... grew into... this."

"I'm pulling over at the next exit," said Alba. "This is ridiculous. We can't have a horse in here!"

"Wow. I've never seen anything like that before in my entire life! That was *amazing*," cried Henry, his mouth gaping open. "You girls should have your own TV show!"

Jax turned to us then. Tears filled her eyes. "Guys, my wish came true. Emily is real. I never thought my wish would come true in a million years!"

"Jax, you wished for Emily to be real?" I asked, wondering if that was what had happened. Had Jax's wish really come true somehow, or was this just a coincidence of epic proportions?

She nodded, sniffling. "Duh. I've been wishing for her to be real ever since I got her when I was a little girl."

I frowned. I didn't understand what was happening.

The RV swerved to the right and the next thing I knew, Alba had pulled us over to the side of the road.

"Shorty, get that thing outta here before it destroys the entire vehicle. Or worse, before it kills someone!" instructed Alba, pointing at the door.

Jax's mouth hung open. "Uh! But, Alba, this is Emily! She's my friend!"

"Come on, Jax," said Holly. "She's a wild animal. She can't be in here. Alba's right. She could hurt someone."

"Mercy?" asked Jax, looking at me like I needed to be the tie breaker.

"I don't know, Jax. She's pretty wild. Let's just get her outside and figure out what to do next."

Jax hung her head, but when Sweets got out the passenger door and opened the back door of the RV, she did what she was supposed to do and led Emily out the door.

The second Emily felt the fresh air on her face, she took off, running and leaping over the nearest fence and into the field along the side of the road. She galloped around excitedly, as if realizing herself that she was real for the first time.

Next to me, Jax clapped and squealed with excitement as she watched her unicorn frolicking about. "I can't believe Emily's real. This is the best day of my life!"

Alba, who had gotten out of the RV and walked around it to stand next to us on the side of the road, grimaced. "Today is the best day of your life, Shorty? Get outta here. Our car broke down. We had to sleep at a truck stop. Our money and all our stuff was stolen. We got a serial killer in the backseat. And today's the best day of your life?"

Tears rolled down Jax's cheeks. "Yeah. I mean, I finally got a real live unicorn!"

Alba shook her head. "Shorty, obviously we're not gonna keep her."

Jax sucked in her breath and stared at Alba. "What do you mean, we're not gonna keep her?! That's Emily! She's mine!"

"The stuffed animal was yours, fine, but that's a real live horse! Where you gonna keep a real live horse? In your room at the B&B?"

Jax was done crying, but she didn't even bother to wipe away the tears that still glimmered in her eyes. She was too mad. "First of all, Emily is a *unicorn*, Alba. And second of all, I don't know where I'll keep her, but I'll figure it out. And third of all, you're not the boss here. Emily is *my* unicorn. And I don't care what you say, she's coming with us!"

"But, Jaxie," said Sweets, her eyes glued to the playful unicorn. "She's having fun out there. What if she doesn't *want* to come with us?"

Jax put both hands on her hips and struck a superhero pose. "Oh, she wants to come with us. Just wait and see." She sucked in a deep breath and then hollered with every-thing she had, "EMILY!"

The unicorn came to a screeching halt, mid-frolic, and looked over at Jax curiously.

"EMILY! Come here!" she hollered, beckoning the horse with a hand.

Emily whinnied and then threw her head back, tossing her rainbow mane into the wind. Then she galloped over to us and stopped right in front of Jax.

Jax smiled and patted her head. "Good girl. Emily. Now

that you've had a little play time, it's time to go. In you go," she instructed.

Emily dipped her head and then calmly walked back into the RV.

All of our jaws dropped.

Jax smiled like a proud mother.

"What?! She *listens* to Jax?" asked Holly.

Jax nodded calmly. "See? She's mine. Now, come on. Let's go. We've got some thieves to catch and a serial killer to return."

CHAPTER 21

Weekend traffic in Baltimore was crazy, and it got even crazier as we neared the Druid Hill Park, where the music festival was being held. With Emily guarding Henry, the five of us crowded up at the front of the RV and peered out the windshield, looking for any signs of the punk rocker kids we'd seen at the truck stop. "Where do we even start looking for them?" asked Alba, driving slowly through the swarms of pedestrians that filled the park area.

"It's going to be next to impossible to find them in all these people," said Sweets.

But then an arm went out. Jax pointed towards the end of a long row of cars. "Is that their van?"

We all squinted and looked in the direction she'd pointed. Sure enough, there was a black van up ahead, but it was hard to tell if it was theirs.

"Only one way to find out," said Alba, turning the RV towards the van.

It took forever to get through the hordes of people flocking to the open-air concert arena. Music and warm air filtered into the open windows, making it feel like summer vacation for the first time since we'd left Aspen Falls. Warm savory scents from the various food vendors around the park filtered into the vehicle too, making me suddenly hungry.

"Ugh, I'm starving," I complained.

Sweets nodded. "I was just thinking the same thing. Maybe after we get the credit card back, we can grab a bite to eat."

"Oooh, I wonder if they have funnel cakes," said Jax. "I love those."

Alba groaned. "Can you guys focus? We have so much on our plates right now and you guys are talking about funnel cakes."

"Alba," said Sweets. "We need to eat. We have to keep up our strength."

"Fine, we'll go through a drive-thru after we drop the murderer off at the police station. Happy?"

"Not really, but—"

I tapped the girls on the shoulders then. We were finally close enough to see the van. "Look! I see the bumper sticker! It's definitely their van!"

"Yay!" squealed Holly. "Now we just have to find them. Park beside them, Alba. So they can't get out of their parking spot."

"Way ahead of you, Cosmo." Alba pulled the RV to a stop right beside their van, which was parallel parked between two other vehicles along the side of a road. There was a second line of cars parked along its driver's-side door, so by us parking on its passenger side, we'd essentially trapped the vehicle on all four sides. Alba shut off the engine and unbuckled her seat belt. "Let's start by searching the truck."

Everyone except Henry and Emily piled out of the RV.

The first outside, Holly tried the doors. "They're locked."

Jax smiled. "Oh, don't worry. I got this." She cupped her hands to her mouth and shouted into the van. "Emily! Can you please come here? I need your help."

Seconds later, Emily was outside, garnering stares from the festival goers.

Jax pointed at the van. "Emily, would you please break the window of this van."

"Jax!" gasped Sweets. "That's destroying property!"

"So? They shouldn't have stolen our things, then! We just want back what's rightfully ours."

I nodded. "I agree with Jax, Sweets. This is on them. They cut our tie-downs and stole our stuff. If they hadn't done that, we wouldn't even be here right now."

Sweets sighed. "Oh, fine."

Jax grinned and nodded at Emily, who promptly head-butted the front passenger window, using her horn to shatter the glass. Jax threw her arms around Emily's neck. "Thank you, Em. You're the best!"

Emily neighed and then walked back into the van. Jax smiled proudly as she looked at us. "You're welcome. Now, if you don't mind grabbing my stuff for me, I'll just go watch Emily and Henry so they don't get into any trouble in the RV."

I reached inside the shattered window and popped the locks on the vehicle. Alba threw open the side door, and we discovered that sure enough, our bags were inside. They'd all been gone through, and now all of our stuff was sprawled around the floor of the van, intermixed with crumpled Taco Bell wrappers and half-used quarts of oil.

Holly's mouth gaped open as she stared at the mess. "Look what they did to my new clothes!"

"They were looking for anything worth money," I said.

Holly began stuffing her clothes back into her back. "It's *all* worth money. Do you know how much some of these things cost?" She held up a particularly filmy blouse and shook it in the air.

"They're dudes," I said with a shrug. "They have no idea. I mean, honestly, *I* don't even have any idea either. To me, it's all just clothes." I looked up to the front. "Sweets, any luck up there finding your wallets?"

From the front seat, Sweets shook her head. "No. But I found a lot of empty Mountain Dew bottles."

Alba, who had crawled clear into the back of the van and was digging through a pile of junk, shouted, "Bingo! Found the wallets."

"You found my wallet?" asked Sweets.

Holly crossed her fingers and pinched her eyes shut. "Please tell me my dad's credit card is in there. Please, please, please!"

Alba flipped open Holly's wallet. Each of the credit card slots was empty. She sighed. "Sorry Cosmo. It's all gone. They took it all out."

Holly's eyes flashed open. "What? All gone?"

Alba handed her the purse. "See for yourself. They even took your IDs. They gotta have the cards on 'em. Finish grabbing your stuff from here, and then we'll go see if we can't hunt 'em down. They gotta be around here somewhere."

While Holly took her time folding her things and putting them back in her bags, Alba, searched everything else in the van just in case the cards were there. Sweets was now seated in the passenger seat of the van, checking all the glove compartments and little nooks and crannies. I found as much of my stuff as I could and stuffed everything back into my backpack, then I did the same with Jax's stuff. When both bags were filled, I heaved the straps onto my shoulder and turned around. And there, standing between me and the RV, was a well-dressed woman with smooth blond hair, a white toothy grin, and a microphone. She stood smiling broadly next to a man holding a video camera.

She reached a hand out to shake mine. "Hello, I'm Vivienne Martin with KELS TV Station, Channel 94 News."

I looked at her curiously. "Hey."

"Derek and I were here in the park covering the festival when someone gave us a tip that there was an RV over here with what appeared to be a real-life unicorn inside. Do you know if this is the RV they were talking about?"

I swallowed hard and gave the media pair a tight smile. "Umm. Unicorn? I honestly don't know what you're—"

"Mercy, are we ready to go yet? Emily's getting restless in here," shouted Jax from the busted-out window of the RV.

The woman gave a bit of a nod to her camera man, and he lifted the business end of his camera towards me and began to film. "So this *is* your RV?" she asked me, holding the microphone up to my mouth.

"No, it's, uh…" I glanced over at Holly, Sweets, and Alba, who were all still inside the van. "Umm, no. It's not our RV. We're just borrowing it."

"But you know who owns it. Is it true that there's a real-life unicorn inside?"

I rubbed the back of my neck. "A real-life unicorn?" I said. I felt heat crawling into my face. Not only had we broken into the van behind us, but we had a serial killer and a unicorn trapped in the RV behind the news station duo. I felt trapped behind a rock and a hard place.

And then before I could think of a proper lie, Jax stuck her head out the broken window. "Mercy. Are you guys done getting all our stuff? Emily *really* wants to come out and play." And then she lowered her voice and whispered. "I think she has to do her business."

My eyes widened and I nodded my head towards the camera crew, trying to send Jax a signal to shut up.

But she just looked at them and smiled. "Oh, hi. I'm Jax."

"Hi, Jax. My name is Vivienne Martin with Channel 94 News. I was wondering if I could speak with you?"

Jax's smile widened. "You want to speak with *me*?!"

"Yes, if you have a moment."

"Sure!" said Jax excitedly. "Hang on. I just have to settle my unicorn down. She's kind of acting like she needs to use the ladies' room."

As Jax disappeared from the window, I bent at the knees slightly, rolling my eyes and throwing my head back. *Jax!* I wanted to scream.

When I resumed my upward position, Vivienne Martin's eyes were on me. "So there *is* a unicorn inside. Can we go in?"

"No!" I shouted. They couldn't go inside. They'd see Henry duct-taped in the kitchen. "No. Jax and Emily will come out here. Just—just stay here."

I ran inside the RV and found Jax in the bathroom. "What are you doing?!"

"Fixing my hair. Does it look okay?"

"No, Jax—"

She frowned and looked in the mirror again. "It doesn't? I thought it was okay."

"No, I didn't mean your hair. I meant, what are you doing telling those reporters that we have a real-life unicorn in here?"

Jax put a hand on her hip. "Why can't I tell them?"

"Because obviously that's drawing attention to ourselves. We don't need attention drawn to ourselves. Henry here is worth ten grand, Jax. What if they figure out this is the RV that they've all been reporting about and that we have the Baltimore Area Serial Killer on board?" I shook my head. "If they show the RV on the news, we'll have people on our tails like crazy."

A hand went to Jax's mouth. "Oh my gosh. I never thought of that. Okay, well, I won't mention a word about Henry, then."

"Look, just take Emily and the reporters over there, away from the van. I'm gonna get Sweets, Alba, and Holly to put all our stuff back inside and then we're going to go find those punks. You're in charge of Emily and Henry. Okay? Can you handle it?"

Jax smiled broadly. "Of course I can handle it! Don't worry. I got everything under control."

Jax's promise didn't exactly instill confidence in me. Regardless, we had work to do. As Jax and I came down the two steps of the RV to the parking lot, Emily followed closely behind us. The camera was already on us.

"Coming to you *live* from Druid Hill Park, this is Vivienne Martin of KELS Channel 94 news, where a real-life unicorn has just been spotted attending the Memorial Day music festival in an *RV*."

With the camera on her and Emily, Jax grinned broadly. I motioned with my head, trying to remind her to get the cameras away from the RV and away from the black van.

Jax took the hint and lead Vivienne Martin and her

camera man towards the grass and away from the RV and van. "Would you like to see her run?" she asked.

"Our viewers would *love* to see her run. Can you tell us her name?"

"Yes, her name is Emily..." Within seconds, Jax and the reporter disappeared around the back of the RV.

I rushed towards the van and stuck my head inside. "Girls. We gotta get outta here. There's a camera crew here. We have to quit messing with this van, and we need to find those guys before someone sees the RV on TV and knows where to find their ten-thousand-dollar meal ticket."

Alba stuck her head outside. "What? There's a camera crew? For what?"

"Someone saw Emily and tipped off a news crew that was here at the park. Jax is out there now, trying to draw their attention away from the RV and all of us. Let's throw all of our stuff in the RV and go find those kids that stole the credit cards."

"What about the killer? We can't leave him alone in there," said Alba.

"Jax said she'd handle it."

"Oh no," Alba balked. "I've learned my lesson where that one's concerned. I can't trust Shorty to do anything right. In fact, she's the reason we're in this predicament right now. If she'd just stayed on the turnpike like she was supposed to, we'd be in Philly looking at a stupid giant paintbrush instead of ransacking a van with a unicorn and a serial killer in an RV."

I glanced over my shoulder at the RV, hoping like heck that reporter didn't come back before we had a chance to get everyone out of the van. "Look, Alba, I don't know what you want me to say. But that news crew could be back any second, and they can't see us coming out of this van with a bunch of stuff or they'll think we're robbing it. We need to get moving."

"Ugh!" Alba groaned, hanging her head. "As much as I'd rather just go with you and help you find those jerks who stole our stuff, I gotta remember my motto. If you want something done right, you do it yourself. So I'll just stay here with Henry."

"You sure?"

"Yeah, you three go. I'll be here with the getaway car ready and waiting."

I shrugged. "Works for me. Hey, Sweets, Holly, come on. We gotta get outta here."

"I'm just looking for the match to this earring," said Holly, scanning the floor for a gold hoop.

"We don't have time for that. If you two want to find your credit cards, we have to go right now."

Sweets got out of the van. "I'm ready."

Holly groaned but climbed down out of the van. "Fine." She handed her stuff to Alba. "Here."

Alba took Holly's bag. "You guys better hurry. We don't have a lot time."

"Come on, girls. Let's go!"

CHAPTER 22

Holly, Sweets, and I pushed our way through the thick crowd. I had absolutely no idea how we were going to find the guys who'd stolen our stuff in a crowd of this size. The place was so huge, it would be like finding a needle in a haystack. There were three different stages, an assortment of food trucks, and various paths to take. We didn't even know which way to go to start.

After walking around aimlessly for several minutes, Holly finally stopped walking and sighed. "This is ridiculous. We're never going to find them like this. There are too many people here, and I can't even see over the person in front of me!"

"Holly's right," said Sweets. "Plus it's hot out here, and I'm starving." She glanced over at a food truck just a few yards away. "Can't we just stop for a little snack? I think my blood sugar's getting low."

"We'll get snacks once we have the credit cards back." I looked around. What we needed was a better vantage point. We needed to have eyes higher than the crowd so we could figure out where we needed to be. Suddenly I came up with an idea. "I got it. Holly, I'm going to lift you up in the sky and fly you around. From up there, you should be able to see things much more clearly. Maybe you'll find those boys from up there."

"But, Mercy!" said Sweets. "People will see her!"

I threw my hands up. "A news crew has already seen Emily, so I honestly don't think a flying girl is going to shock anyone today. Besides, we have no choice. We're running out of time. We still have to get Henry to the police station and then we have to get our car before seven. Otherwise we're stuck in Baltimore until Tuesday, and Alba will miss her brother's wedding. If that happens, we'll never hear the end of it!"

Holly let her arms fall to her sides. She arched her back and, with her eyes closed, she stuck her nose into the air. "Fine. Fly me. I'm ready."

Thankful that she wasn't going to pitch a fit, I pulled her backwards towards a tree so we could have a little privacy while I prepared to launch her into the air. I flexed my fingers and inhaled a deep breath. "Give me a thumbs-up if you see something, and I'll bring you down. Okay?"

Holly nodded.

"Be careful, Holly," said Sweets, giving her a quick hug.

"It's not me that needs to be careful." Holly turned to me, her face completely serious. "Please don't drop me. Okay?"

Anxiety was already eating away at the insides of my stomach. While my powers of telekinesis were getting better, they certainly weren't to the point of being flawless like Alba's were. I gave Holly a crooked grin. "I'll do my best." Closing my eyes, I worked to absorb as much energy from the living things around me as I could. Then, with a flick of my finger, I had her off the ground, focusing all my concentration only on her and tuning out the crowd around me.

For Holly's part, she was a good sport about it. She pressed her lips together to keep from screaming and drawing attention to herself. And when I got her high enough in the air, she abstained from flapping her arms to steady her balance and moving too wildly for me to keep ahold of. Instead, she kept her body rigid and her breathing steady and she did what I needed her to do, which was to put her trust in me.

Sweets watched her with an eagle eye as I moved her around the crowd, looking for signal she might throw our way.

To begin, I moved Holly to the nearest stage, the first of three. I had to be careful not to move her too quickly, as she needed to scan the crowd as much as possible before I could move her to the next location. When she was done searching there, she pointed to the west.

"She's ready for you to move her, Mercy," said Sweets. She pointed in the direction Holly had requested. I moved her, following her instructions. Shockingly, I didn't hear any screams telling the world that there was a flying girl in the sky. I wondered if perhaps she'd actually managed to go unnoticed.

When she got to the second stage, I let her hover near it for several seconds, before sweeping her slowly across the crowd. At one point, she held up a flattened palm.

"Oooh, she wants you to stop!" said Sweets.

I froze her there, letting her hang. Then, suddenly, she put up a thumb. Unsure if we'd be able to find that exact position if I reeled her back to us, I held her in the air while I walked, something I hadn't ever done before. "Sweets, guide me through the crowd," I instructed. "I can't take my focus off Holly or I might drop her."

Sweets understood immediately and took my elbow. "I got you, Mercy. Here we go."

Together the two of us walked through the crowd. Sweets was my eyes on the ground while I kept my eyes to the sky. Finally, we stood near Holly. From up above, she pointed towards a banner hanging across the stage. It read "The Punk Heroes of Baltimore"! This was the stage! If we were going to find them, this was where they were the most likely to be.

When Holly saw us nearby, she motioned with her hand. She wanted us to move her around again. I did as she asked until she once again gave a thumbs-up. This time, she beckoned us animatedly.

Sweets and I rushed to get closer while I moved Holly closer to a tree so I could gently lower her without being noticed. When she was safely on the ground, I let out my breath. That might have been the longest I'd ever held anything up in the air by myself in my life. It had almost completely worn me out, and I suddenly wished we had those snacks Sweets had been asking about. But there was no time for that. We had work to do. We rushed to be by Holly's side.

Her eyes were wide as she came at us. "I saw them! They're over here!"

She grabbed us both by the arm and tugged us through the crowd, then stopped suddenly and pointed through a break in the crowd. Sure enough, the three guys we were looking for sat together in a crowd with a bunch of other teens and twenty-something kids with colored spiky hair, face jewelry, and studded clothes. They had a big plaid blanket spread out across the grass and were all lounging around on it, munching on snacks and laughing and talking.

"It's them!" said Sweets.

"So what do we do?" asked Holly, nibbling on her nails.

"I don't know," I whispered back. Were we just supposed to go up to them and confront them? Or would that prove to be too much of a challenge? They probably wouldn't give us the cards back if we just asked for them anyway. I stared at the group, trying to think of all the possible options. As I looked them all up and down, I noticed one of the guys had his wallet attached to a chain and stuffed in his back pocket. That gave me an idea. "Holly, see that one there, on the end?"

"Yeah?"

"Look. His wallet's on a chain. I think I might be able to use my powers to lift it out of his pocket, but it's attached to his pants. Can you go over there and wait for it? I'll lift it as high as I can get it and you go through it."

Holly's blue eyes widened. "Seriously? What if they catch me?"

Sweets linked arms with her. "Don't worry, Holl. I'll go with you and be your bodyguard."

Holly looked up at Sweets, her forehead wrinkled. "No offense, Sweets, but what are you going to do to save me? Bake them into muffins?"

Sweets giggled. "If I need to."

I rolled my eyes. My energy was quickly draining. I didn't know if I even had enough in me to do another lift, but we had no choice. Making jokes certainly wasn't doing anything to conserve the little amount of energy I had left. "Just go. We're running out of time."

Sensing I was serious, Sweets and Holly both raised their brows before cowering together. They pressed their way through the remaining people between us and the guys on the blanket, positioning themselves just off to the side and behind the man with the wallet. When Holly shot me a look, I nodded and then flicked my finger at the wallet. It moved a bit in the man's back pocket. I held my breath, hoping he wouldn't feel the movement. Feeling like Holly and Sweets could be busted at any second, my heart raced in my chest. But I pressed ahead, and slowly, the wallet slid upwards. At one point, the man did reach around and scratch his backside, so I froze any movement. He didn't seem to notice his wallet was now midway out of his pocket, and he made no effort to push it back down, though he did shift his position on the blanket, making it easier for the wallet to slide out.

Finally, it was out and, though attached to a chain, it managed to float a foot or so into the air. While it hovered there, Holly and Sweets slid down to the grass with their backs to the men. They sat cross-legged behind them, and Holly hooked an arm over the top of the chain, so the wallet was in front of her.

"Hurry, Holly, hurry," I whispered to myself. I was afraid both of my powers failing me and of them being caught.

It took only seconds for her to flip through the wallet and to discover that there was no sign of the missing credit cards. She glanced up at me and shook her head.

Darn! I sighed as I watched Holly put the wallet down on the blanket behind the man. Then she pointed at the man next to the one we'd just checked. He was in a more difficult position. He faced me. I couldn't see his backside, so I couldn't see his wallet. I lifted my hands in an overly dramatic shrug. If she wanted to check that wallet, she'd have to lift it out herself. I pointed at her.

Her eyes widened and she pointed at herself.

I nodded.

Then she leaned over and whispered something in Sweets' ear. When Sweets crawled to her knees, I knew it was on. They were going to do it themselves.

I held my breath as I watched. First Holly made sure her two top buttons were wide open, then she fluffed her hair before fluffing her breasts. Shaking my head, I couldn't help but smile. She was going to flirt her way to his wallet!

She stood up. Took two steps away from the guys, pulled out her phone and pretended to be speaking on it. Then she walked towards them, pretending to be oblivious to them and tripped over her own feet, diving right into the pile of boys. She giggled when she landed, and I could see her mouth move. "Oh my gosh! How embarrassing. I'm sorry."

The guys all pulled back at first, surprised to have the intrusion, but when they realized they had a busty blond in their midst, they immediately leaned forward to help sit her up. Sweets used that exact moment to pluck the wallet out of the man's back pocket. It was quick and effortless, like taking candy from a baby.

From where I stood, I watched as Sweets opened the wallet and peered inside. When her brows shot up and a smile curved the corners of her mouth, I knew we had the right one. But no sooner had Sweets figured out we had the right wallet than one of the men frowned at Holly.

"Hey, I recognize you. You were at that truck stop this morning."

Holly's eyes widened just as the man whose wallet Sweets had stolen, turned around to see Sweets kneeling up closely behind him.

He saw her holding his wallet in her hands. "Hey!" he hollered. "That's my wallet!"

My eyes widened as Sweets tried to climb to her feet. *Oh no!* Knowing there was no way that Sweets could outrun the guy, I flicked a finger out, shooting Sweets up into the air.

"What the—?!" His neck cranked up to see Sweets suspended in the air.

"This was a setup!" he cried, turning to look down at Holly.

My heart beat faster. I didn't care who saw. I flicked a finger at Holly next, sending her up into the air beside Sweets. In any normal instance, I don't think I could have lifted both of them, especially after being so weak, but my adrenaline was racing. I was sure this was the burst of superhuman strength one got in times of emergencies.

"Look!" cried several people around them.

With no time to lose, I flew Holly and Sweets over everyone's heads as fingers all began pointing skyward. No one seemed to notice me standing there, quietly controlling their movements like the ultimate puppet master. When I'd gotten Holly and Sweets as far as I could manage to hold them, I felt my powers begin to weaken. I felt faint, like I could pass out at any minute. I had to get them to the ground without dropping them. Slowly, I lowered them, but when they got several feet above the ground, my powers gave out. I felt the energy disappear, and I knew I'd dropped them, though they were too far away and there was too much crowd separating me from them that I didn't know how they'd landed or if they were alright.

All I knew was that I needed to get back to them.

The guys that had been on the blanket were already on their feet and weaving their way through the crowd towards Sweets and Holly. My heart raced, making me feel even more light-headed. I tried to push my way through the crowd, but I felt like I was walking in a spinning tunnel. All the lights and sounds made me dizzy and nauseous. I suddenly felt like there was no way I was making it back to the RV, but I pushed on.

I made it almost all the way to the path that Sweets and I had walked in on when I felt my knees buckle. I stumbled over my own feet and felt myself fall to the grass. On my hands and knees now, I fought to get back up again. But no matter how hard I tried, my body was too weak. There was no way I was getting back up again. I reached out in front of me, when suddenly, the whole world went dark.

CHAPTER 23

A cool breeze caught my hair and whipped around my face. My eyes fluttered open, and I discovered I was riding on the air. Panicking, my whole body flinched, and I looked down. The green park and the people below me all looked small as I flew past. Fingers pointed at me, and I could hear the tiny shouts of onlookers.

"Look at that!"

"There's another girl flying!"

"Hurry, get your camera. There's another one!"

How in the world was I flying like this? I had no idea what had happened. The last thing I remembered was chasing after Holly and Sweets and collapsing in the middle of the park. And now I was sky-high and moving towards our parking spot at a very fast rate. But where was Holly? Where was Sweets? And where were the punk rockers chasing after them?

When I saw that I was over the green near our parking spot, I felt myself slowing and little by little getting closer and closer to the ground. I tried to get my feet under me, but I still felt like a newborn deer, wobbly and weak. So when I finally did touch down, I sank like a rock into the grass. But thankfully, out of nowhere, Alba appeared.

"Get up," she hollered at me.

"I can't. I'm too weak. Where are Holly and Sweets?"

"They're a little ways behind you. We gotta get you in the RV before they show up. I have to take care of those guys chasing them. You don't think you can get in the RV yourself?"

I shook my head. "No, I don't think so. I'm spent."

Alba put two fingers in her mouth and let out an ear-piercing whistle. "Wait here. I gotta go help the girls."

"But—"

"Just wait here, Red. Help is on the way."

I sighed and lay back in the grass while Alba took off in a dead sprint towards the park. My eyes closed. I felt so tired. Suddenly, I heard pounding on the ground.

"Mercy?" called Jax's voice in the distance. "Oh my gosh, Mercy!"

I pinched one eye open and saw a horse's white muzzle looking down at me and then Jax's face over it. She was riding Emily. "Jax…"

Jax scurried down off Emily and rushed to my side. "Are you hurt?"

"I had to use my magic. I'm weak. I can't walk," I whispered.

"Don't worry, I'll help you." She hooked her hands underneath my armpits and managed to get me up on my butt. Then, with her help, I managed to get to my feet.

"Emily, help Mercy, please," she begged, her squeaky voice filled with panic.

Emily let out a whinny before kneeling down on the ground so Jax could help me climb on. Then Jax got on behind me and held on to Emily's mane while she got to her feet.

"Back to the RV, Em."

Emily pivoted around and trotted towards the RV.

"Where are Alba and the rest of the girls?" asked Jax. "She went to find you."

"We got caught. Holly and Sweets were being followed by the guys who stole our stuff."

Jax sucked in her breath. She made a little clicking sound, and Emily ran faster. She galloped past the van, where glass still lay scattered around its tires, and then pulled up to a stop in front of the RV. Jax made another little clicking sound and Emily climbed the RV's two steps, and then we were back inside the RV. Henry was seated at the table, still bound. "You're back. Did you find what was stolen from you?"

"I don't know," I said. "Jax, I need something to eat. I'm weak."

"Got it." Sniffling, Jax threw a leg over Emily's back and slid down onto the sofa. Then she tugged on me, making me collapse onto the sofa next to her. She smiled up at the unicorn. "Thanks, Em."

She immediately began rifling through the kitchen cupboards in search of something edible. "There's some crackers in here."

"Sure," I said, holding my hand out. Anything would work, I was sure. I was just so completely out of fuel.

Screaming outside caught my attention. I could see out the window on the opposite side of the RV and to the van. Sweets and Holly were running like mad towards us.

"Start the car! Start the car!" screamed Sweets.

"Jax!" I hollered. "They want us to start the car. I can't—"

Jax tossed me the sleeve of crackers she'd found as she raced past. Jumping into the front seat, she started the engine just as Holly and Sweets flew inside. "Where's Alba?"

"She's dealing with those guys that were chasing us!" panted Holly, out of breath from the long run back to the RV.

I shoved a cracker in my mouth and then watched out the window as Alba appeared out of the crowd, a group of guys following closely behind her, screaming at her.

She stopped once to turn around and flick a finger at the mob following her. In one fell swoop, she managed to sweep all their feet out from underneath them, and they fell to the ground. She kept running and within a split second they were almost all on their feet again. She ran past their van, waving at us. "Go! Go! Go!"

But the guys were almost at her again. One of them stopped and looked appalled when he saw the broken glass scattered on the pavement. "My van! What did you do to my van!" he hollered.

Alba jumped into the vehicle as it started to roll away.

But the angry mob followed, shouting at all of us. "They destroyed my van!"

"Stop them!"

Standing in the doorway of the moving RV, Alba flicked another finger at them, firing a bright burst of electrical energy towards them and sending them all reeling backwards into a pile.

"Zap their tires!" shouted Henry, his brown eyes ablaze with excitement.

Alba fired at each of the tires in turn, zapping them all flat and melting them to the road. Then she turned to Jax. "Go, Shorty, go! Get us outta here!"

But the roads were still clogged with pedestrians trying to get to the festival and cars circling the area, trying to find empty parking spots. Jax was forced to take the RV onto the grass, tearing up the lawn as we peeled away. Alba kept her head out the window, waiting to fire at anyone that tried to follow us, but thanks to their van not having tires that worked, we managed to get out of the park without them on our tail. Getting back onto the interstate was a breeze as it was literally just off the park.

Now that we'd made our getaway, Alba fell into the seat across from Henry, breathing heavily. "Oh my gosh, that was intense. Those guys were ticked!"

"That's because we stole their wallet," said Sweets, pulling the man's wallet out of her pocket and waving it in the air.

"You got it!" said Jax, turning almost all the way around in the driver's seat and clapping her hands excitedly.

Alba pointed a finger backwards at Jax. "Eyes on the road and two hands on the wheel, Shorty."

Jax's eyes grew big as she turned back around and put both hands on the steering wheel. "Guys, where are we going? I need to know where to go."

Holly pulled her phone out of her bra. "I'll find out where the nearest police station is."

Alba lifted her chin towards Sweets. "So are yours and Cosmo's cards in there?"

Sweets shot Alba a huge smile. "Everything's in there. My cards, Holly's dad's black card, and both of our IDs. It was all there."

Alba smiled too. "Well, that's a relief. I gotta hand it to you girls, you did good."

Sweets pointed at me just as I shoved another cracker into my mouth. "It was all Mercy. She lifted Holly in the air so we could find them. Then she lifted the first wallet out, and when they busted us for pickpocketing, she's the one that got us out of there before anything bad could happen."

Alba nodded at me. "Way to go, Red. Nice lifts."

I shrugged and choked down my dry cracker. "Holly's the one that made it possible for Sweets to get the second wallet. I just got them out of there in time."

"Yeah, Holly did good too," agreed Sweets.

"Alright, I'll give credit where credit's due. Nice goin', Cosmo," said Alba.

"Thank you," she said pluckily while staring at her phone. "Jax, which direction are we headed?"

"I took the I-83 South exit," said Jax.

Holly made a face. "Shoot. We need to be going north."

"Okay, I'll get us turned around as soon as I can," said Jax.

"I've never been this drained before," I said to Alba. "I don't get it. You do lifts and fire energy all the time, and I've never seen you this spent."

"You gotta understand, Red. I've been doin' this for years. Eventually your body kinda adapts and you start conserving energy better. Plus we really haven't eaten much. That's the main thing." Then she turned and hollered up at Jax. "Hey, Shorty, when you get off the interstate to turn around, why don't you pull this rig over to the next drive-thru you find? We might be at the cop shop for a while. We should all eat before we get there."

Jax saluted Alba in her rearview. "Aye-aye, Captain."

CHAPTER 24

J ax pulled the RV off the interstate into a little commercial area with fast-food restaurants and a little strip mall. Scotty Bee's Burgers, a fast-food chain with a big waving bumblebee as its mascot, was the first place to greet us. And since its parking lot was nearly empty, Jax pulled in.

"Drive-thru, or are we going inside?" asked Jax, wiping her nose with a piece of toilet paper.

"Going inside," said Holly. "I need to use the ladies' room."

"We got a bathroom right here," said Alba, pointing to the back of the vehicle as Jax pulled the RV to a stop along the outer curb.

Holly wrinkled her nose and looked at Alba like she was crazy. "Ew. I'm not going in there. Have you seen that bathroom? It's disgusting."

Alba rolled her eyes. "Whatever. But you better hurry up. We're running out of time."

"I know, I know," sang Holly as she stood up. "Anyone else coming in?"

"Me!" said Sweets and Jax simultaneously.

"Not me," I said. "I don't have it in me. But can you get me a cheeseburger and fries and a chocolate milkshake?"

"Sure. Alba, you want anything?" asked Holly, straightening her blouse.

"Same as Red."

"'Kay. How about you, Henry? You want something to eat?"

Henry's eyes widened, and a smile spread across his face. "I'd take what everyone else is having, too. If you don't mind."

Holly smiled at him. "I don't mind."

"What about Emily?" asked Jax, looking at the unicorn standing in the rear of the RV.

"What do unicorns eat?" asked Holly.

Jax shrugged. "Rainbow sprinkles?"

"Eh, doubtful," said Alba, pinching one eye shut. "They're like cousins to horses. Whatever a horse would eat, a unicorn's gonna eat."

"Okay, so like carrots?" suggested Jax.

Holly rolled her eyes. "Fine. We'll see if they have any carrots. Come on, girls. Let's go."

When they were out of the vehicle, Henry looked at Alba. "I don't suppose you'd consider cutting me out of this tape so I can use the facilities?"

Alba looked over at me. "Whaddaya think, Red? Can we trust him?"

"Yeah, cut him loose," I said. "He's not going anywhere. Emily's back there."

Alba lowered her brows and looked at him sternly. "You know we're witches, right?"

Henry's head bobbed up and down. "Oh yes. I know, I know."

"So there's no point in trying to escape."

"I swear. I'll be good. This is the most fun I've had in years. I don't wanna go anywhere."

Alba stood up and walked over to stand in front of him. "Well, don't get too excited. Our next stop is the police station to turn you in and collect our reward."

Henry lifted his brows as Alba cut the duct tape binding his arms down. "Oh no, I understand completely." He rubbed his wrists. "Oh, that feels so much better. Thank you!" She removed the tape from his ankles, giving him the ability to finally stand up normally. Leaning against the table, he kicked out a leg and flexed his foot and ankle and then switched sides and did the same. "So much better," he repeated before heading to the bathroom.

Minutes later, Jax, Holly, and Sweets returned to the RV with a big bumblebee-printed to-go bag and a tray of milkshakes for us and a garden salad for Emily. We spent the next five minutes devouring our food and discussing how close we were to finally getting out of the situation we were in and how thankful we were that we'd finally be back on the road by nightfall.

After I'd eaten almost all of my food and was just finishing the last of my shake, I was finally beginning to feel like myself again when there was a knock on our RV door.

Everyone looked around curiously.

"Who in the world is that?" asked Sweets.

Alba stood up, but before answering the door, she looked back at Sweets. "Hey, Sweets, you up for driving?"

Sweets' head bobbed up and down, her eyes big.

"Good. Get up there, will ya?" She looked around the RV. "No one else moves a muscle. Got it?"

We all nodded as Sweets got behind the wheel and Alba went to the door. Whoever it was knocked again.

Tearing the door open, Alba looked down to see a man and a woman in their midfifties standing on the pavement staring up at her. "Yeah?"

The man, who was a little overweight with a skunk-colored beard and close-set eyes, put a hand up to hold on to the handrail on the RV. "Yeah, we, uh, we saw the camper on the news earlier." He cleared his throat. "We're here for Henry."

Alba's eyes widened as her head tipped sideways. "Excuse me?"

The man tried to poke his head into the camper. "You got him, don'tcha?"

My heart began pumping wildly. Just as we'd feared. Someone had spotted the camper on the news and wanted Henry for the reward money.

But Alba wasn't having it. She shoved the man back by the shoulders. "No, I don't know who you're talking about, and how about you don't go poking your head in where it don't belong?"

That got the man upset. He tried to shove his way past Alba and into the RV. "Henry!" he shouted.

I glanced over at Henry. Wide-eyed, he'd slunk down low in his seat.

"Drive, Sweets," I hollered as Alba wrestled with the man. "Hang on, Alba."

Sweets tore out of our parking spot.

The motion separated Alba and the man, but as he fell, he was able to grab hold of the RV's steps, and we dragged the man several feet. When she had her balance, Alba flicked her finger and fired a shot of energy at him, but somehow he managed to hang on until Sweets rounded the corner out of the parking lot and he flew off, rolling over several times before landing flat on his stomach.

Alba slammed the door shut and we all went to the window, where we could see him scrambling to his feet. Both he and the woman he was with climbed into an old green Cutlass and tore off after us.

"They're following us!" shouted Jax, racing to the back of the RV to throw her arms around Emily's neck.

"Hurry, get back on the interstate, Sweets," said Alba.

"O-okay," said Sweets, her eyes scanning her mirrors. Taking the first exit, she glanced in her mirror again. "They're still back there!"

"We'll have to shake 'em," said Alba. As soon as we were on the interstate, she pointed to the other lane. "Switch lanes. Get in front of that semi up there!"

Sweets did her best to weave through traffic, but the Cutlass wove through traffic too, easily keeping up with us. No matter what Sweets did to shake them, they kept up with us. Finally, Alba was forced to stick her head out the window. When they got right behind us, she fired at their tires, trying to take their car out, but her electrical bursts kept coming up short, and when they realized what she was doing, they learned to swerve whenever they saw her head out the window.

Finally, back inside, Alba sat down on the seat. "It's no use. They're too far back, and I keep missing."

Emily let out a whinny and stomped her foot down on the floor, shifting nervously, as if she could feel the nervous tension in the air. Her tail shot out, smacking against the old curtains covering the back window. The motion kicked up a cloud of dust into the air.

Wiggling her nose, Jax sniffled. "Emily, no, it's okay. Relax," she cooed, trying hard to calm her.

But Emily was still upset about the chase. She swatted the curtains again with her tail, sending more dust into the air. This time, Jax couldn't hold back. She let out a huge sneeze, all over the Scotty Bee's bag lying on the kitchen counter.

Within a matter of seconds, a horde of buzzing bumble-bees erupted from the bag, filling the whole RV.

"Jax!" cried Holly. "What did you do?"

Jax's eyes were wild as she stared at the bees swarming her head. "I—I don't know. I just *sneezed*."

I waved my hands around my head as the bees began to attack me.

The bees swarmed Emily's head and body too, making her shift about crazily in the kitchen.

"Sweets!" I hollered. "We have a bee infestation back here."

Sweets looked in her rearview mirror. All of our arms flailed about wildly, and Emily was tossing her head from side to side. "What do I do?"

"You're gonna have to pull over," shouted Holly, trying to cover her head with a pillow from the sofa.

"We can't pull over," said Alba. "Those people will catch up to us!"

"We have no choice," hollered Jax. "Emily is freaking out."

"I'm pulling over," said Sweets, putting on her signal light.

"Sweets, no!" Alba, still being swarmed by bees, raced to the front of the vehicle to stop Sweets.

As bees swarmed her, Emily moved about wildly. She bucked her head, and Jax had to duck to keep from being hit by her horn. When she missed, the horn stabbed through the side of the RV's walls.

"Ahhh!" screamed Jax. "Right now, Sweets! Emily's going wild!"

Ignoring Alba's protests, Sweets pulled over as fast as she could. And the second the RV came to a stop, Jax rushed to open the camper door and Emily went sprinting out, followed by Jax. Holly and Sweets both went out next, screaming. Alba and I helped Henry to his feet, and the group of us bolted out the side door, all the while swatting bees from our heads.

Outside we found Emily galloping up and down the shoulder, trying to lose the few bees that had followed her outside. But standing there then, I realized that Sweets hadn't gotten us completely off the interstate. Half of our RV was still in the right lane. Cars zoomed past, honking their horns and being forced to swerve into the left lane. But before we had time to get in and move the RV, the Cutlass that had been following us pulled up behind us.

The man got out of his vehicle and started towards us. Alba held her finger up at him, as a warning. "Stay right there!" she hollered.

He put a hand behind his back and pulled out a gun, just as a blaring horn made us all turn around. Two semis were coming up fast, side by side, and there was no way one of them was moving in time.

"Run!" I hollered, pulling Alba and Henry's arms and throwing all of us down into the ditch only seconds before the semi sideswiped our RV, obliterating the driver's side and sending pieces of it flying all around us.

CHAPTER 25

When the noises all finally stopped, I uncovered my head. Henry and Alba were on either side of me with their heads covered. Further up the embankment, Jax, Sweets, and Holly stood staring at the wreckage with their mouths hanging open. I turned around and sat up to see that our entire RV had been destroyed, and the semi that hit it had kept right on going. No cars even bothered to stop along the busy section of the interstate. The clothes that we'd gathered from the van at the Druid Hill Park were now scattered all over the ditch along with pieces of the RV.

I turned back to see that the man in the Cutlass had gone to the ground too. He was on his hands and knees now, crawling around, apparently searching for the gun he'd lost when he'd fallen.

"Alba, that guy's trying to find his gun," I hissed. "We gotta get out of here!"

Alba uncovered her head and looked over in the man's direction. Sure enough, he'd already gotten his gun and was on his feet. He held it out in front of himself as he strode towards us.

"Henry!" he hollered. "You're coming with us!"

"I'm not going anywhere with you!" Henry hollered back, trying to climb the side of the embankment.

"Emily!" hollered Jax. "Help!"

"Look," the man began as the woman in the passenger seat got out of the car and started towards the group too, "we're not going to hurt any of you. We just want Henry."

"Sure you do," said Alba. "And the ten large that comes with him!"

"Ten large?" said the man, narrowing his eyes.

Galloping now, Emily was almost upon us. Jax pointed at the man. "Get him, Emily!"

Emily rode past Alba, Henry, and me. Her rainbow mane whipped around her shoulders, making her look both magical and regal. She was almost to the man when he pulled the trigger.

"Emily!" screamed Jax as a gunshot rang out. "Nooooo!"

The noise sounded muffled as it dug into Emily's chest and she fell to the ground.

"Noooo!" screamed Jax rushing to be by Emily's side.

The man looked down at his gun, seemingly in shock that he'd actually pulled the trigger.

No sooner had Jax gotten to Emily than the unicorn began to make a hissing sound and her body began to shrink. It was as if she was deflating. In seconds, what had been a regal, galloping unicorn was now nothing more than a stuffed animal once again. Tears streaked down Jax's face. "You killed Emily!"

"I…" said the man, his mouth gaping open.

But before he or the woman could do anything else, Alba flicked her finger at the man, sending his gun flying out of his hand while simultaneously sending their car somersaulting backwards until it finally landed on its top. Then with her finger, she lifted the couple up into the air and put them up in a tree several yards away. She wiped her hands together. "There, that oughta keep 'em out of our hair for a while."

All of us girls rushed over to be by Jax's side as she sobbed over the loss of her friend.

"Jax—" I began, unsure of what to say.

"He killed Emily!" she sobbed, her shoulders shaking.

"She saved us, Jax," said Sweets. "Emily's a hero."

"I know, but now she's gone!"

Though all of our hearts were heavy as we watched Jax mourn the loss of her unicorn friend, I knew we weren't safe on the side of the road. Too much traffic zipped past us. We had to get to a safe place, and we were running out of time. We had to get Henry to the police station, and then we had to get back to the truck stop. Alba and I hooked our arms under Jax's elbows and brought her up to her feet. She clung to Emily, now only a stuffed animal once again.

"Jax, I'm sorry," I whispered as I hugged her. "But we have to get out of here. We can't stay here. It's not safe."

"How are we supposed to get anywhere?" asked Sweets. "We just lost our ride!"

"And all my clothes!" said Holly sadly.

I pointed at the Cutlass. "We could've taken their car, but now it's a smashed potato. Good going, Alba."

Alba flicked her finger again and the car rolled back onto its tires. The roof was almost entirely caved in. The sides and doors were dented, and several of the windows had been busted out. There was no way that thing was ever driving again. Alba palmed her forehead. "Ugh. Well, that was dumb."

Holly flipped her hair over her shoulder and sucked in her breath as if she was going to say something.

I pointed a finger at her. "Don't even go there, Holly."

She put her hands on her hips. "What? I was just going to say that I'll find us a ride."

"Yeah, right," said Alba, rolling her eyes.

Holly frowned. "I'm serious, Alba. That's all I was going to say."

Alba shrugged and then did a little half bow, sweeping her arm out in front of her. "Alright, then, be my guest. Get us a ride, Cosmo."

"Gladly." Holly adjusted her top, straightened her skirt, and fluffed her hair. Then she walked to the side of the rode and stuck out her thumb.

"Oh yeah, like that's gonna work," said Alba, shaking her head. "Little do you know, Cosmo. That kind of crap only works in the movies."

Undaunted, Holly fanned her face with her free hand as she kept her thumb out. Within minutes, a pickup pulled over to the side of the road. A twenty-something-year-old man wearing blue jeans and an Orioles ball cap got out and walked around to look at the mess scattered around the ditch. "You ladies need some help?"

"Someone hit our RV," said Holly, plumping out her bottom lip.

"I see that. Didn't they stop?"

She shook her head and did her best to look sad about it. Her blond hair blew around her face in the wind. "Nuh-uh."

"Well, that's terrible. Where you headed?"

"To the nearest police station. Think you could give us a ride?"

The man nodded his head towards Henry. "He your grandfather or something?"

Holly nodded. "Yup. We were just taking Grandpa here out for a little weekend adventure, but there were some bees in our camper, and when we pulled over to let them out, a semitruck came out of nowhere and smashed it all to bits."

The man pointed at the car behind us. "That your car too?"

Holly's eyes widened. "Ummm."

"No, that's not our car," said Alba. "That was here when we pulled over."

"Huh. Must be a dangerous part of the interstate," said the man.

Holly giggled at him. "Must be." She held out her hand to him. "I'm Holly, by the way."

He shook her hand. "Jake."

Holly gave him one of her best smiles. "Hi, Jake, it's a pleasure to meet you. So do you think you could give us a ride to the police station? We need to report all of this."

"Yeah, I can give you a ride. I don't have room for all of you up front, though. Maybe just you and your grandfather."

Holly linked arms with Jake and together they began walking towards his truck. She flipped her hair over her shoulder as she looked back at us. "That's fine. My friends can sit in the back. They don't mind. Do you, girls?"

Alba groaned. "No. Of course not. Not a bit."

I had to suppress a smile as Sweets and I hooked arms with Jax. "We'll take care of Jax. Alba, you get *Grandpa*."

Alba sighed but took hold of Henry's elbow. "Fine. Come on, *Grandpa*. Time to go."

~

BY THE TIME we got to the police station, Jax's face was red and swollen from a combination of crying and her allergies. But we'd managed to calm her down, and she was mostly done with the tears. We all unloaded from the back of Jake's truck, and Alba went around to the side to help Henry slide out.

"Thanks for the ride, Jake!" said Holly as she scooted out last and slammed his door shut.

Jake leaned over the steering wheel and looked at all of us standing there. "You girls have plans after this? There's a music festival going on over at Druid Hill Park. I was just on my way home from work to change and then I'm meeting some friends over there later this evening."

Holly tipped her head slightly. "Oh, I really wish we could, but we've got lots of stuff we have to do after this. You know, get our ride figured out and everything. But we really appreciate you getting us this far."

"Yeah, thanks, Jake. We owe you one," I added, giving him a wave.

"No problem. Glad I could help. Oh, hey…" He held out a finger and then grabbed an old receipt inside his center console and scribbled something down on a piece of paper and held it out the window. "Here's my number, in case you get into any more jams and need help. Or in case you change your mind about later."

"You're so sweet, Jake," said Holly. "Thank you."

He nodded. "Good luck getting home." He waved at us as he drove away, and we were left staring up at the police station.

Finally we'd made it.

Flanking Henry on his left and with Alba on his right, I

looked down at him. "Well, I guess this is the end of the road, Henry."

Henry looked disappointed that after everything, the trip was coming to an end. "You sure you don't want to go do something else exciting?"

Alba lifted her brows. "Trust us. This was plenty of excitement for one day. We have to go get our car out of the shop by seven so we can keep on the road."

"Come on, girls. It's almost six now," said Sweets.

We walked into the police station in a big group and went right up to the front desk where a uniformed police woman sat doing paperwork.

"Hello. We need to speak to a police officer," I said.

The policewoman looked up from her work. "Yes?"

I glanced over at Alba. She gave a little nod. I cleared my throat and continued. "We need to speak to someone about collecting the reward money for the Baltimore Area Truck Stop Killer."

She frowned. "Collecting the reward money? That's for information leading to his capture. We haven't captured him yet."

Alba shoved her way past Jax and Holly and to the woman's desk. "We've got more than just information. We've got the guy right here."

The officer, a brunette with her hair pulled back into a slick bun and a name badge that read Officer Jorgensen, looked at us curiously. "Who? That guy?"

"Yup," said Alba, shoving Henry forward. "That'll be ten grand. We prefer cash."

Just then, the front door of the police station flew open and the man and the woman that Alba had put up a tree came barreling inside with a policeman. "There they are! Arrest them!"

CHAPTER 26

Our jaws all dropped.

"Arrest *us*?!" shouted Alba. "Arrest *them*! They tried to steal this guy from us so they could gather the reward money."

The woman who'd been chasing us stepped forward. "What reward money are you talking about? There was no reward money offered."

"Yes, there is," said Holly. "We heard it on the radio. It's ten thousand dollars."

The man with the salt-and-pepper beard lifted his brows and shook his head. "Sorry to disappoint you girls, but Henry ain't worth ten grand."

With a hand on her hip, Alba turned to look at the police woman. "Tell these people that the Baltimore Area Truck Stop Killer has a reward offered."

The police woman stood up. By now, several other police officers that had been milling around the area were now standing in the front, all listening to what was going on. "Well. Yes, you're right. There *is* a ten-thousand-dollar reward issued for information leading to the arrest of the truck stop serial killer."

Alba crossed her arms over her chest and smirked at the man and woman. "*Thank* you."

"Except, *that's* not the truck stop serial killer," said the policewoman.

The girls and I all froze in stunned disbelief. "What?!" we all said in unison.

The man who'd been chasing us quirked a smile. "You girls thought *Henry* was the truck stop serial killer?!" He shook his head. "Whatever gave you that idea?"

I pointed at Henry. "I saw his picture and his RV on the news this morning."

"And that meant he was a killer?"

"Well, we heard the radio announcement about the truck stop killer. He fit the description," I added, feeling suddenly nauseous.

"How? Because they're both men?"

"They said he walks with a limp…"

"I'd be willing to bet that a large percentage of the old people in Baltimore walk with a limp," said the man.

"And they showed the RV!" I said. "I know it was the same guy."

"Look, I'm not arguing with you. Henry was definitely on the news," said the man.

"And I happen to know that Henry was scared and running from someone," added Holly.

"Well, that's also very true. He was running from us!" The man pointed to the woman. "Look, Henry *was* on the news a couple of times, but *not* because he's the truck stop killer. He went missing from his assisted living home last night. We've been looking for him all day. He stole a parked

RV and took off with it. We've been trying to find him ever since."

The woman nodded and stepped forward. "Henry's my father. We've been worried sick about him."

We all stared at Henry then.

"This is your daughter, Henry?" asked Jax.

Henry hung his head, looking embarrassed. He gave a barely visible nod. "Yes. That's Katie. She's my daughter. And that's her husband, Dave."

"Henry!" gasped Jax. "Why didn't you tell us?!"

"Well, I tried to tell you that I wasn't the truck stop killer, but you didn't believe me, and then after a while, I was having so much fun with you that I didn't *want* to leave because then I knew you'd send me back to the home, and it's so *boring* there. I just wanted to have a little fun."

Alba palmed her forehead. "Henry! I can't believe you punked us!"

Henry wagged a finger in the air. "I didn't punk you girls. You were the ones that threw me in the RV and took off. Now, I'm sorry you aren't going to get your reward money, but it's really not my fault. I *did* tell you I wasn't the person you were looking for."

Alba shook her head. "I just don't understand. He really seemed to fit the description we heard on the radio. If Henry's not the killer, then who is?"

The policewoman went back to her desk, pulled a sheet of paper from a stack on her desk and handed it to Alba. It was a fuzzy picture of a tall man with a beard, wearing a baseball cap. Though perhaps there were certain bits of his face that resembled Henry's, it was clearly not the same person, though something looked vaguely familiar about the photograph. Officer Jorgensen pointed at the picture. "That's the photo we've released to the media. It's a bit grainy as it was pulled from surveillance video footage, but that's the man we're looking for."

And then, suddenly, Jax sucked in her breath. She looked up at all of us, a grin on her face. "I recognize him! I recognize this man!"

Officer Jorgensen looked interested then. "You do? Do you have identifying information about him?"

Jax shook her head. "No, but I saw him." She turned to look at me and Alba. "At the truck stop. This morning, when we first got there. There was a man coming out. He had a red baseball cap on and a beard. He held the door open for us."

My eyes widened. Of course! I remembered him now too! "Yes! Jax! You're right. I remember him." I pointed at the photo. "I'm sure of it. That was the guy!"

And suddenly, I knew what we had to do. "Girls. We have to go." I glanced over at Henry. "Henry, I'm so sorry. But we have to go now."

But Henry's son-in-law, Dave, wasn't about to let us leave. He took a step towards us. "Now wait just a darned minute. You ruined my car! That was a vintage Cutlass! I've put a lot of time and money into restoring it. It'll cost thousands to put it back to how it was."

"But you pulled a gun on us!" countered Jax. "And you shot Emily!"

"Emily?" asked Officer Jorgensen.

Dave, furrowed his brows. "Their weird-looking horse. I-I don't know what happened…"

"You *killed* her. That's what happened. And she wasn't a horse, she was a—"

"Stuffed animal," chimed in Alba, firmly. "She was a stuffed animal. And never mind all of that. We have somewhere else we need to be. So, we're sorry about your car.

That was an accident." Alba tried to leave, but Dave slid in her way.

"Officer, I want these girls arrested for the abduction of my father-in-law and for the damage they did to my vehicle."

All of us girls gasped. None of us could believe what was happening. We were trying to do something for the *good* of society and take a serial killer off the streets of Baltimore, and now we were going to be punished for trying to be helpful?

Alba shook her head. "Oh, no. You're not gonna pin all of that on us. It's not *our* fault. You shouldn't have pulled a gun on us. We were defending ourselves."

"It *is* your fault. You ruined two vehicles. The RV that Henry stole, and my car. Not to mention the fact that you damn near scared the daylights out of my father-in-law."

Henry waved his hands in the air. "Oh no. I had the best time of my life with these girls! In fact, I'd prefer to go back and spend the rest of my time with *them* rather than to have to go back to that boring nursing home."

"But, Dad!" said Katie. "They take really good care of you there."

"Katie, that place is where people go to wait to die. I have too much life left in me to go to a place like that."

Katie sighed. "Dad, I didn't know you felt that way. Why didn't you ever tell me that was how you felt?"

"I've tried!" said Henry, his brow wrinkling. "No one wants to listen to me!"

Katie wiped away the tears from her eyes. "Well, I'm listening now. You can come home with Dave and me, and we'll figure something out. Would that make you happy, Dad?"

Henry looked excited. "Really? You mean it?"

She nodded. "Of course I do. I don't want you to be unhappy. I love you."

The girls and I tried to inch our way out the front door of the police station without anyone noticing, but Dave was way ahead of us, blocking our exit.

"Oh no. This isn't just about Henry. This is about my car!" He looked at Officer Jorgensen. "These girls need to pay for what they've done to my car!"

It was my turn to take a stand. I pressed my way to the front of the group so I could stare down Dave. "Look. Here's the deal, Dave. You want your car fixed? Well, we need to have money in order to do that. If you press charges and put us in jail right now, then it's gonna take years for you to squeeze a penny out of us. We're all broke college students on a road trip. Our car broke down and we don't have two nickels to rub together, let alone money to fix *your* car."

"Yeah!" interjected Jax. "That's why we we're doing this anyway—to raise money to fix *our* car."

"But if you let us go, there's a chance we could find the *real* truck stop killer and get that reward money, which would go a long way towards fixing your car."

"What about the RV?" asked Katie. "Dad stole the RV, but it was your fault that it got smashed."

I sighed. I had no idea how much it was going to cost to fix an old Cutlass and an RV. But I knew we didn't have a shot at doing any of it without that reward money. "Let's cross that bridge when we get to it. Right now, there's still a chance we could find the real killer. But if we wait *too* long, he could get out of the area."

Officer Jorgensen shook her head. "I don't understand. How do you feel so confident about finding our guy? Do you know where he's hiding out?"

"It's kind of a long story, and it'll take too long to explain it all to you, but look, we found Henry, didn't we? All we need is a chance. If we don't find him, then we'll give you our information and I guess you can send us a bill, and we'll pay it off over the next ten years. *Or* you can give us a minute and we'll see if we can't get that money for your sooner."

Dave made a grunting noise. "Lemme talk to my wife. Hang on." He took Katie by the elbow and pulled her off to the side. They spoke in hushed whispers for a minute and then turned back around again. "Oh, fine. You've got until the end of the day, and if you don't have that reward money in hand, we're pressing charges."

I rubbed my hands together. "We'll do our best." Looking over my shoulder, I smiled at my friends. "Let's go, girls. We have work to do."

CHAPTER 27

I t was six forty when the police van dropped us back off at the Dusty Trucker's Roadside Emporium. In exchange for being allowed to leave, the police had taken down all of our contact information just in case we decided to try and skip town without making good on our promises. At that point, we felt a sense of urgency. With jail time looming if we didn't get the reward and take care of our financial obligations to Henry's family, the stakes were higher than they had been all day. We felt that we had no choice but to track down the man we'd seen in the wee hours of the morning and figure out a way to turn him in to the police.

But first thing was first. We couldn't very well hunt down the *real* truck stop killer without a vehicle. So as soon as the police left, we walked around to the side of the building, hoping that our vehicle was finally done. We found it parked outside of Phil's shop.

"Phil, we're back," said Alba. "Please tell us our car's done."

Phil, who'd been standing in front of a tool bench

working on some kind of part, turned around and cracked a smile. "Well, good! I'm glad to see you're back!" He nodded towards the clock hanging on the wall. "I was starting to get a little worried that you weren't going to be here before closing time."

Alba waved her hand in the air like it was no big deal. "Nah, we just had to run an errand. No big deal. So, is the car done or not?"

Phil wiped his hands off on a blue shop rag he'd pulled from his pocket. "Oh, it's done alright. It's been done since five like I promised it would be."

"Awesome," said Alba, smiling.

A huge smile covered my face too. Just knowing we had our very own transportation again, meant we were going to get out of this horrible mess we were in. *Eventually*. I moved to the side, so Holly could go forward. "Pay the man, Holl."

Hesitantly, Holly walked forward. "I thought we were gonna use some of the reward money to pay for the car to get fixed."

"Oh, we are," said Alba. "But, obviously, we need the car back before we can go earn that reward money."

Holly plucked her dad's black card out from where she'd stashed it in her bra, but before handing it to Phil, she asked, "Excuse me, Phil? Wouldn't you prefer cash to a credit card?"

He shrugged. "If you've got cash, I'd certainly take it."

"Well, we don't *have* the cash just yet, but we're supposed to go pick it up soon. But we can't pick it up without our car. Is there any possible way that we could use the car to go get the cash and then bring it back to pay you?"

Phil let out a little chuckle. "Sorry, miss, but that's not how it works. You don't get the car until it's paid for."

Holly frowned. "Well, how about this? I'll give you my card numbers, and if we're not back with the cash by later today, then you can charge my card."

Phil winced. "I'm getting ready to close up shop for the evening, and I'm not open again until Tuesday. There's no way you'd be able to get me my cash until then, and as far as I understand, y'all are itching to get back on the road."

"We are!" agreed Alba, lifting her brows and looking at Holly with contempt.

Holly's eyes scanned the area. "Look. We'll put the cash in an envelope and hide it anywhere you want. It'll be here when you open up on Tuesday morning. If we fail and it's not here, *then* you can charge my card."

"You don't understand. I have to charge your card in order to know that you've got the funds available to cover the repairs. I'm sorry. I can't wait to do that until Tuesday morning."

"But if you found the money here—"

"Look, the best I could do for you would be if I found the money here on Tuesday morning, I could refund your card. Okay?"

Holly thought about it for a second. "Yeah, I guess that would work. My dad might not even notice that the charge was ever there. Where do you want us to hide the money?"

He pointed to a mail slot in the door. "No one else will be in or out of here all weekend. Just put it through the mail slot."

"Will do! So, what's the total of the repairs?"

He walked over to his little wooden counter and punched a couple of numbers into a greasy old-fashioned register. "With parts, labor, and tax, it comes to eight fifty."

"Oh man, our reward money is dwindling fast," said Alba, frowning.

"Hey, if we're able to get back on the road even-steven, then I consider this whole thing a win," I said.

"Me too," said Sweets, nodding.

"Me three," agreed Jax.

"Fine, whatever. But let's get it paid for so we can get on the road, huh?" asked Alba.

Holly flipped her card across the counter to Phil. "Here ya go, Phil. Charge it."

~

WHEN PHIL HAD BEEN PAID, we all rushed around Sweets' car, chattering excitedly.

Sweets was the first one in. She caressed her steering wheel before giving it a little hug. "Oh, it's so good to have you back. Mommy missed you!"

"I gotta admit, it feels *amazing* to have her back," I agreed. "Now we can work on finding the real killer and get the heck outta Dodge."

"I second that motion," said Alba. She looked at me then. "So, what's your brilliant plan for finding the real killer?"

"Well, I'm not promising it will work, but it kind of all depends on Holly."

"On Cosmo? Oh geez. We're all doomed," said Alba, rolling her eyes.

I elbowed her. "Hey, be nice. Holly's had a lot of valuable input into everything we've done on this trip."

"That's debatable."

I leaned forward to Holly, who'd called shotgun. "Don't listen to her, Holl. I've got faith in you." I turned my head. "Sweets, can you drive around and park right in front of the building?"

"Sure."

As Sweets pulled the car around, I began to explain my idea.

"Look, when we got here super early this morning, we all saw the real killer. You guys remember?"

Sweets pulled into the parking spot right in front of the building. "I remember. The guy was coming out just as we were going in."

"Exactly. And he held the door open for us," I said.

"Okay?" said Jax, shaking her head and frowning.

"He *touched* the door."

And then Holly's eyes widened. "He did *touch* the door! Oh my gosh. I never thought of that. If I touch the door, I might be able to see where he's at. Just like I did with those guys that stole our stuff!"

I pointed at her. "Bingo."

"Well, what are we waiting around for?" asked Alba. "Cosmo needs to touch that door!"

CHAPTER 28

"We'll catch you if you fall, Holly, don't worry," I assured her.

Standing next to the truck stop's front door, Holly let out a puff of air and nodded. "Okay. Here goes nothing." She placed her hand on the door, while Alba and I stood ready to catch her. At first, she appeared unaffected, but as she slid her hand slowly down the length of the door, she found the spot he'd touched and immediately, her face went blank.

"Ahhh, it's working," squealed Jax.

"Shhh," I hissed back. "Let her concentrate. We can't afford for her to break her concentration."

Jax pinched her lips between her teeth and nodded reverently.

We all watched quietly as Holly's body flinched and then went limp in Alba's arms. More than a minute passed before finally, she began to moan.

"Holly!" I said lightly, trying to help her out of her trance. "Holly. You okay?"

Holly's eye lids fluttered open. But before she could

even suck in a deep breath, we noticed that tears filled her eyes. "Oh, girls!" she breathed. "It's going to happen again. The killer is going to strike. I saw him. He was with a woman. He's got her! We've got to get to her before it's too late!"

"Where, Holly? Where are they?" asked Sweets.

Tears streamed down Holly's cheeks then as she shook her head. "I don't know. I couldn't tell. It was dark, and I got the sense it was cool. Like a garage or a cellar or something. The woman is so afraid, I felt her fear."

"So what do we do?" I asked.

"Help me up." Holly tried to stand, but her legs were weak. "Inside."

Alba and I hooked our arms under her elbows and got her to her feet, and with Jax and Sweets holding the doors, we got her inside to Rick's Diner, where we took the nearest table.

"I'll get you something to drink, Holly," I said and rushed to the counter, where Rick was still working. "Hi, Rick, I need an orange juice, please."

"Sure thing. Hey, I'm glad you're back. I've got your paychecks ready for you," he said as he set about getting a tall slim glass from beneath the counter.

"Oh, good. Thanks."

"Yeah, no problem." He looked over at the table, where Alba, Sweets, and Jax all crowded around Holly. "Everything okay?"

I shrugged. "I don't know. We're trying to find someone before it's too late."

Rick frowned as he poured orange juice into the glass. "Find who before what's too late?"

I leaned across the counter then. "Can you keep a secret?"

He looked around the diner. "I'm here alone again. Who am I gonna tell?"

"Have you seen or heard anything on the news about the Baltimore Area Truck Stop Killer?"

"The guy killing people and leaving two-dollar bills as his calling card? Yeah, I literally just heard a thing on the news a few minutes ago. Creepy, huh? Why?"

"We think we saw him here earlier this morning. When we first got here. My friend has some psychic tendencies. She has this feeling there's another woman in danger right now. She's kind of upset about it. The juice is for her."

Rick looked down at the juice he'd just poured and slid it across to me. "Oh, here, here. Give it to her."

"Thanks. I'll be right back up to pay for it."

"Yeah, no problem."

I took the glass over to Holly and handed it to her. "Here, Holl." I looked at Sweets. "Has she said anything else that would be helpful?"

Sweets shook her head. "No. Nothing. She's too upset."

I rubbed Holly's back and went back to the counter to pay for the juice. I handed Rick a five.

He took the bill. "You sure the guy on the news was the same guy that you saw earlier?"

I nodded. "We saw a picture of him. I *know* it was him."

Rick put the five in his drawer and then tipped his head to the side curiously as he pulled out my two dollars and change. "You know, I had a guy in super early this morning that paid for his breakfast with a five and a two-dollar bill."

My eyes widened as he handed me the change. "Was it an older guy wearing a red baseball cap?"

Rick winced. "I honestly didn't pay a lot of attention to what he looked like, but yeah, I think it was an older guy."

"Rick, do you still have the two-dollar bill he gave you?"

"Yeah." He pulled out his wallet and showed it to me.

I held up the two one-dollar bills Rick had given me as change. "Can I have that bill?"

He shrugged. "Well, it's dumb, but I sorta collect two-dollar bills."

"Please, Rick. If that bill was from the serial killer, I think my friend might be able to use it to find him."

"Yeah? How does she do that?"

I shook my head. I didn't have time to get into all of that. "She just can. Like I said, she's got psychic tendencies. Please?"

"Yeah, I suppose. I mean, if it gets this whack job off the street, how could I not?" He exchanged bills with me. "Here ya go. Good luck."

"Thanks."

I took the bill over to the girls and sat down at the table. "Girls. You're never going to believe what I just got." I held up the two-dollar bill.

"Yeah? What's the big deal?" asked Alba.

"Do you remember what the news report we heard this afternoon said about the serial killer?"

Sweets' eyes widened and she sucked in her breath. "He's leaving two-dollar bills as his calling card!"

I nodded as a smile crept across my face. "Yup. And Rick said an old guy was in this morning and paid for his breakfast with this."

"You mean, that was the killer's?!" asked Jax, staring at the bill in horror.

"I think so. Listen, I have a plan. But I need a few things from the convenience store. Come on."

～

MINUTES LATER, armed with a map of the greater Baltimore area, four white candles emblazoned with a Baltimore crab sticker on them, Sweets' gold necklace, and the killer's two-dollar bill, we all sat at the table in the middle of Rick's Diner.

"Oh my gosh, I sure hope this works this time," said Jax, setting each of the candles on the map in the four cardinal directions.

"It has to work," agreed Holly, her eyes still rimmed with red. "That poor woman's life depends on it."

Sweets held her necklace up over the map as we'd done in the van. When it stopped swinging, she glanced up at us and gave a little nod.

I swallowed hard and began the chant.

> *"Keeper of Lost and Missing Things,*
> *Unlock the magic which this item brings.*
> *Its rightful owner can't be found,*
> *The time has come to look around.*
> *Whether by the mountains, sea, or snow,*
> *We don't know which way to go.*
> *So take this object which once was theirs,*
> *And on this map, show us where*
> *We will find them, where they'll be.*
> *Their just karma is our destiny.*
> *So point the necklace and stop its swing,*
> *Oh Keeper of Lost and Missing things."*

At the end of the chant, the necklace began to sway. Getting excited, we repeated the chant in unison several more times, whipping the necklace up into a swirling tizzy until the radius of the circle it spun in got smaller and smaller. Eventually, it pinpointed one tiny area along the interstate, just outside of Baltimore.

"There it is, girls," whispered Sweets.

"I'll call Officer Jorgensen and let her know what we've figured out. I'll have her meet us there," said Alba.

Holly nibbled on her fingernails. "Let's just hope that woman is still alive when we get there!"

CHAPTER 29

The ExpressLane Truck Stop was a short fifteen-mile drive away from the Dusty Trucker's Roadside Emporium. One phone call to Officer Jorgensen set a whole lot of wheels in motion, and we were given strict instructions not to go into the ExpressLane until her team was assembled and on site. So in the meantime, we sat just across the road in the parking lot of an abandoned pancake house, waiting for them to show up.

"This is totally freaking me out right now," said Jax, gnawing on her fingernails as we all stared at the Express-Lane Truck Stop on the other side of the road.

"You and me both," agreed Sweets.

"I'm just worried that we're going to be too late to save that woman," said Holly. Her teary eyes scanned the roads all around us, looking for the police brigade that was supposedly on its way. "I wonder what's taking them so long?"

"It hasn't been that long. I'm sure they're coming as fast as they can," I said.

"It's not like they're just sending some rookie cop out

here to handle a shoplifter or something. This is a serial killer they're dealin' with," said Alba. "They gotta be ready to handle anything."

Holly nodded. "Yeah, I know. I'm just worried about her. She was so scared. I could feel it. I hate not being able to help her."

"Holly, you are helping her. We're here. And hopefully we're going to be able to save her," I said.

We sat for only another couple of minutes before an ambulance and several police cars showed up with zero fanfare. They'd left off the sirens and the lights, presumably so as not to alert the killer that they were coming for him.

One of the police cars pulled up to the passenger side of Sweets' car. Holly rolled down her window to see Officer Jorgensen riding shotgun with a large uniformed man behind the wheel.

She rolled down her window. "Hey. We were glad to get your call." She nodded towards the gas station across the street. "So you think he's there?"

Holly let out the sigh she'd been holding. "I sure hope so. I think he's got a woman with him."

Officer Jorgensen nodded. "That's why we've got the ambulance here. Just in case. It sure would be nice to know how exactly you girls know all of this."

"It's a really long story," said Holly. "We don't have time for it right now."

"*Really* long," agreed Jax.

"And right now I'm just worried about getting over there and saving that woman."

The officer nodded. "Agreed. Alright, so do you know where exactly we should look?"

"I kind of have a feeling, but I'm not entirely sure. The girls and I are going to drive over there and ask a few questions about the layout of the building. Maybe that'll spark something for me."

Officer Jorgensen shook her head. "No, that's too risky. You girls stay here. We'll handle it."

"But you don't know what you're looking for," said Alba. "*We* know what we're looking for."

"That's why if you'd just tell us…"

Holly shook her head. "No. We have to do this. Look, when we know where he's hiding, we'll gladly tell you. It's not like we're trying to confront a serial killer if we don't have to. But you going barging in there is only going to alert him that you're onto him. Then he might kill her. I can't let that happen."

Alba patted Holly on the shoulder. "*None of us* are gonna let that happen."

Officer Jorgensen sighed. She looked over at her partner sitting next to her. Then she leaned her head back, and the two of them whispered back and forth for a few moments. When they were done talking, she opened up her glove compartment, pulled out a small pair of binoculars and held them up to look at the truck stop. Adjusting the lenses, she slowly swept them along the front of the building. Finally, she put them down.

"Fine. We'll let you go inside. The second you know anything, I want you to wave at me. I can see you from here just fine. When we see the wave, we'll come over. Alright?"

Holly nodded. "It shouldn't take us long. Be ready."

WE PARKED in front of the ExpressLane Truck Stop and went inside. It was a smaller station than Dusty Trucker's, only because it didn't have the diner attached, but it was still a hopping place. Truckers came and went from both the front entrance and the side entrance. There was a steady stream of traffic to the bathrooms. And there were three registers open at the counter, each with a line of at least two to three customers in them.

The girls and I picked the line which looked like it would be the shortest wait. It was being run by a young woman with a shaved purple head, a full-color sleeve tattoo on one arm, and a nose ring. When it was our turn at the counter, I was the one to speak. "Excuse me. Can you tell me if you have a cellar in this building?"

The twenty-something woman looked confused. "A what?"

"A cellar. You know, like a basement."

She shrugged. Her listless green eyes looked like either she'd been working too long or she'd stayed up too late the night before. "Oh. I got no clue." She looked around us at the next person in line.

Alba leaned forward. "Think you can ask someone? It's important."

The woman looked annoyed but leaned over to the register next to her and whispered something in the woman's ear. That woman shook her head, and the purple-headed woman stood up straight again only to shake her head too. "Nope. No cellar."

"You guys have like a garage anywhere? Somewhere dark and cool," said Alba.

Purple-headed girl shrugged. "No clue." She looked around us again. "Next."

"W-w-wait," said Alba. She grabbed a candy bar from the front of the counter and threw it in front of the register.

"One fifty-nine," said the woman's monotone voice.

Alba gave her some cash. "Okay, I'm gonna ask you one

more time, and this time I'd like you to think about it for a second. Are there any garages around here?"

The girl sighed. "There's a storage facility in the back, if that's what you mean."

Holly's face lit up. "That's gotta be it!" She rushed out the door to Sweets' car.

"Where at exactly?" asked Alba.

The woman leaned forward and hooked her thumb to the right. "Just around that side of the building all the way in the back."

"Thanks," said Alba, taking her change.

We all rushed outside to find Holly already seated in the front seat of Sweets' car. The rest of us loaded up too and drove around to the back of the building.

That was when we saw it.

A little red pickup truck. Parked in front of the storage building.

"Girls!" I gasped, grabbing hold of the two seats in front of me. I pointed at the red truck. "That truck was parked in front of Dusty Trucker's early this morning when we got there."

"You sure, Red?"

"One hundred percent sure. It was parked next to that black van. I'd recognize it anywhere."

A slow grin spread across Alba's face. "Well then it's gotta be the killer's. I think it's time to let the professionals take it from here."

"I agree," I said. We pulled the car to a stop, and Jax ran out of the vehicle and waved at the cops, staring at us in their binoculars from the parking lot across the street.

Within seconds, the ExpressLane Truck Stop's parking lot was flooded with cop cars. Officer Jorgensen and her partner pulled up next to us. "You know where he is?"

"That's his truck," said Jax, pointing at the truck parked near the storage unit.

"We think he's inside one of the units," said Holly. "But we don't know which one."

The officer nodded and turned to talk to her partner. He said something into his radio while she turned to talk to us again. "We're on it. Thanks for your help. You girls stay back here and let us handle it." She gave a nod to her partner, and he drove them away.

We waited outside in our car. It was completely silent as we held our breath and watched the storage building, waiting for any signs of the serial killer or his victim.

The minutes ticked by on the clock, ratcheting up our nerves with each progressive click.

And then, gunshots rang out in the parking lot.

We all froze.

CHAPTER 30

Jax clung to my arm.

A tear rolled down Holly's cheeks.

"I hope that woman is okay," whispered Sweets finally, breaking the tension in the air.

"Me too," I whispered.

Within seconds of hearing the gunshot, the ambulance pulled up to the front of the building, just as police officers came filing out of the storage facility, causing a commotion.

"Should we go see what's going on?" asked Alba.

"Officer Jorgensen told us to stay here," said Jax, still clinging to my arm.

"Yeah, well, it looks like they've got things under control now. Come on. I gotta know what's going on."

"Me too," I agreed. "Let's go see."

We all unpiled from the car and walked up to the building just as the EMTs wheeled someone out on a stretcher and put them in the ambulance. A few minutes later, two officers came out, hanging on to a man in hand-cuffs. It was the man we'd seen that morning. His face was contorted into an angry snarl. His hair was wild, and he fought the police at every step.

Seeing a real live serial killer made my heart race faster. It made me realize then and there how dangerous it had been abducting Henry. What if he'd actually been a real serial killer? Though I wondered whether, if we'd met *this guy* at Rick's Diner, we'd have actually tried to abduct him. Henry had been an easy target.

Officer Jorgensen came out of the building next. She said something to her partner and then walked over to us.

"You got him, huh?" said Alba, nodding in the hand-cuffed man's direction.

Officer Jorgensen's head bobbed. "Yes. Thanks to you girls, we got him. You just saved some lives."

"What were the gunshots we heard?" asked Jax, sniffling.

"Is it that woman? Is she alive? Is she alright?" asked Holly.

"He did have a woman with him. You girls saved her life. She's a little banged up, but she's alright. We got here just in time. He fired at our officers, but we were able to restrain him before he hurt anyone. He's in custody now."

"Oh thank God," whispered Holly, falling backwards against Sweets.

Sweets and Alba caught her arm and held her up. "You alright, Holly?"

Holly sagged but managed to stand back up on her own two feet. "Yeah, I'm just relieved. I was so worried."

"Now, do you mind telling me how you knew all of this was happening?" asked the officer.

"You wouldn't believe us," I said.

"Try me."

"How about we tell you down at the police station while

you're making out our reward check?" suggested Alba with a grin.

"Yeah, about that. I'm not quite sure you all understand how a reward works."

Alba wagged her finger. "Oh no. I understand how it works. You offered a reward if someone found your guy. We did it. We found him. We also saved a woman's life in the process. And we were promised a reward. There's no backin' out now."

Officer Jorgensen put a hand on both hips and cracked a smile. "I'm not trying to back out. It's just that reward checks aren't just lying around back at the station. There's a whole process we have to go through in order to get one of those approved. It takes a while."

Alba lowered her brows. "A while? Like how long?"

She shrugged. "Sixty days. Sometimes ninety days. It depends on each case."

Alba pointed at the building. "This is an open-and-shut case. We found the guy and we saved a woman's life!"

"I know you did. And we all appreciate the courage it took you to come forward with the information. But I can't just cut you a check. It's not up to me. There's a lot of red tape involved in a process like this. Now, look, we'll go back to the station. I'll take down all your information, and we'll send you the reward money when it gets approved. That's the best I can do."

"But what about Henry's family?" I asked. "Dave and Katie, they want us to pay for their car and for that RV that got hit."

She winced. "I'm sorry, but that's a completely separate matter. These two things aren't related at all."

"But they said they'd press charges against us if we didn't come through with the reward money today!" said

215

Jax. "We can't go to jail. We're trying to get our friend back to New Jersey in time for her brother's wedding this weekend!"

"I'm sorry, ladies. I don't know what else to tell you. You destroyed two vehicles. Someone has to be held responsible for the damages."

"Yeah, but none of that was intentional! We were trying to solve this case!" said Alba. "Isn't there something you can do to help us?"

"I mean, if you had some way to pay for the damages, I think they'd drop any charges they were considering filing. Their concern is getting their vehicle fixed and making sure their father isn't liable for the damages done to the RV he stole."

"But he's the one that stole it!" said Alba. "We were just riding along with him."

Officer Jorgensen offered a tight smile. "Look, I get it. You did a good deed, but the fact remains that someone's gotta pay for the damages. Dave's not going to let you off the hook, I'll tell you right now."

Alba's shoulders slumped. "Well, we don't *have* any money."

Holly sighed. "We've got my dad's black card."

"Holly, we can't let you use that," said Sweets. "I've got a little money in my bank account." She turned to look at Officer Jorgensen. "How much do you think it's going to cost to repair the two vehicles."

"After you left, Dave said something about having it valued recently at twenty-five thousand."

"Dollars?!" screeched Sweets, her eyes wide.

Officer Jorgensen nodded. "And I have no idea how much the RV was valued at. We'll have to contact the owner."

"Well, I certainly don't have twenty-five thousand dollars in my bank account," said Sweets. "I should have enough to pay off the repairs to my car, but I won't have much more than that."

Holly sighed. "I don't know what else to do, girls. If we don't have some way of paying for this, we'll go to jail. I can't go to jail! Do you know what they do to girls like me in jail?"

"No, what?" asked Jax.

Holly pulled her head back and ran a hand through her hair. "Well. I don't exactly know, but I'm sure it's not good." She handed Officer Jorgensen her dad's black card. "Just put all the damages on there. There's no limit, so it should cover everything." She turned to look at us. "I'll just have to deal with my dad when I get to California. I can't have all of us going to jail."

"We'll have the cops send your dad the reward money to help out," said Alba. "At least it's something."

"And we can all work this summer to pitch in and help you with the rest," said Jax.

"Yeah, I'm up for pitching in," I agreed. "Things should've never gotten this far."

Holly shook her head. "No, it's okay. It's *my* dad. I'll handle everything. If I have to work for him this summer to pay things off, then I'll do it. I need to be more responsible."

Officer Jorgensen took the credit card from Holly. "I'll send it back to you when both the repairs on the RV and the Cutlass have been finished. I think this will be enough to keep Dave and the owner of the RV from pressing charges. If you girls want to meet me back at the station, we'll get the request paperwork started for the reward money."

"Before we go, can we see her? Can we see the woman?" asked Holly.

Officer Jorgensen gave Holly a tight smile. "We can see if she'd be up to seeing you."

Holly nodded.

"Okay. Gimme a second."

When the officer left, Holly looked at us. "I know we're in a hurry to get back on the road, girls. But I have to see her. I have to know that this was all worth it. I have to know she's okay before we go." She glanced up at Alba. Alba was the one that was in a hurry to go.

"No, I understand, Cosmo. It's alright. I wanna make sure she's alright too. Come on. Let's go check on her."

We walked over to the ambulance, where Officer Jorgensen was speaking with the woman, who was still lying on a stretcher. Then she nodded and looked up at us, giving us a little curl of her finger.

"Ladies, this is Elizabeth Brown. She's the woman you saved today. Elizabeth, these are the young women who gave us the tip about where you were."

Tears streamed down Elizabeth's face as she reached out and took hold of Holly's hand. "How did you know? How did you know he had me and how to find me?"

Holly wiped away her own tears with her free hand. "It's hard to explain, but pretty much I just had a feeling. Like a premonition."

"But you—you *knew* where to find us. How?"

Holly shook her head and looked down at her hand as she held on to Elizabeth's. "I don't know how exactly. But I'm thankful that we figured it out, and I'm thankful that you're safe."

Elizabeth pulled Holly to her and gave her a hug. Together the two women cried together.

I wiped away the tears in my own eyes and noticed the rest of the girls, including Alba, doing the same. It was an emotional moment to know that we'd saved someone *before* they become just another homicide we had to solve. It felt good. It made me want to try harder in school, and it made me want to be a better detective. It became kind of a defining moment in my life. It was in that moment that I realized I wanted to help *save* people's lives, not just solve their murders.

When Elizabeth finally let go of Holly, she smiled through her tears at all of us. "Thank you, ladies. I don't understand how you did it. Maybe I never will. But you saved my life. He was about to kill me and *you* saved me. I'll never forget what you did for me."

CHAPTER 31

The sun had already set for the day when we drove away from the police station after having settled everything related to the destruction of property charges and abduction charges. We'd also had to make good on our promise to explain to Officer Jorgensen exactly how we'd known where to find the killer and how we'd known that he'd had a woman with him. Of course, she'd not believed us when we'd told her the truth. But then we'd revealed to her that the unicorn spotting and the reports of flying girls in Druid Hill Park were us also. This had prompted a little demonstration of our powers, at which point she'd been *forced* to believe us.

"On the road again," I said, settling back into Sweets' car. I didn't know about the rest of the girls, but after the day that we'd had, I was ready for a nap.

"It's going to be a late night," said Sweets, letting out a little yawn as she pulled her car away from the curb.

"Yeah, it is," agreed Jax, battling her own yawn as well. "What a day. We were up so late last night, running around on high speed all day, and now a long night drive to New

Jersey. Ugh. We're going to have to take half-hour driving shifts so no one falls asleep behind the wheel."

"Or we could just stay in Baltimore for the evening," I suggested with a shrug. "I still have a little cash left."

"And I have my debit card back," said Sweets. "I could get us a room somewhere."

"We *did* get invited to go back down to the music festival and hang out with Jake and his friends," said Holly, a glimmer of excitement shining in her eyes.

We all looked at Alba, who was seated in the passenger's seat. She was staring out the window as we were all talking.

"Of course we'd have to leave first thing in the morning," said Sweets, her face somber.

"But at least it would give us all a chance to shower and look nice when we pull into Jersey City," I said lightly. I knew Alba would want to look nice when she saw Tony for the first time since Christmas. "But if you're not up for it, Alba, we can just drive through the night. Can't we, girls?"

"Oh, yeah. For sure," said Sweets with a nod.

"Mm-hmm. Definitely," agreed Jax, stifling another yawn.

"A shower *would* be nice," said Holly. "I feel gross. But I'll do whatever the majority wants."

Without moving her head, Alba sighed. "I saw a motel over by the festival grounds. It's right along the interstate. I suppose that would be the best place to stay if we're staying."

I glanced to my right and saw Jax winding up to let out a squeal. I shot her a warning look that said *do not do it*. Then I leaned back in my seat, put my hands behind my head, and smirked. "Yeah. That'd be cool. Great idea, Alba."

CHAPTER 32

The next morning, after devouring a large, free continental breakfast in the hotel lobby's dining room, we all loaded back up into Sweets' car and took off. We'd all had a chance to shower, though several of us didn't have any clean clothes to change into as we'd lost it all in the RV. But our spirits were high.

We'd had a great evening, listening to music and hanging around with Jake, his roommate, and a few of their buddies. They had us laughing and enjoying ourselves all evening. It'd been a beautiful summer night. The stars were out and the temperature was perfect. The band was a popular local country-rock band that everyone seemed to enjoy, and we'd all gotten up to dance. The guys had even managed to convince Alba to get up and dance, and they'd spun her around the grass a few times.

So when we finally took off that morning, the whole mood was lighter than it had been the entire trip. We all felt closer together than we had since moving into the B&B. I think the realization that the end of our time together was nearing had finally hit us.

As we drove away, Alba looked back over her shoulder at Jax, who sat quietly clinging to Emily and looking out the window as we got back on the interstate. "Hey, Shorty, you got any more music in your backpack?"

Jax's eyes widened. "Really?"

"Eh, why not?"

With fervent excitement, Jax dug through her backpack, pulling out random items and setting them on my lap and Holly's. Finally, she plucked out a CD and handed it to Alba. "This one was supposed to be for the ride home, but it'll work."

Alba put the CD in, and soon the familiar sound of a synthesized keyboard pretending to be a trumpet playing filled the air. *Da-na-na-na. Da-na-na-naa. Da-na-na-na.* Alba leaned her head back on the seat rest. "Really, Shorty?"

Jax giggled. "I told you. It was for the ride home."

When the lyrics started, we all joined in. "We're leaving together…"

The whole car erupted in laughs as we all suddenly became rock stars for the band Europe, playing the drums and the keyboard on every open surface. And then ended with… "It's the final countdown!"

"Why couldn't you have made the first CD like *this*?" said Alba, smiling when the song was over.

Jax smiled. "Because this is a return trip song. It's the final countdown to us being apart for the rest of the summer."

"Oh, girls, it's going to such a long and boring summer without all of you," said Holly, plumping out her bottom lip. "And my dad's gonna have a conniption when he finds out I charged the repair of both vehicles on his black card."

"Let us help you pay for it, Holl," I said. "With my job at the restaurant, I should be able to pitch in."

"Yeah, me too," agreed Jax.

"We all will," said Alba. "It shouldn't all have to be your responsibility."

Holly tipped her head back. "It's okay, girls. It's time I took financial responsibility. I've decided I'm going to get a job this summer. I'll work for my dad or something, and I'll pay off the debt. It'll be okay. Eventually."

Feeling something moving in my lap, I looked down curiously. The plastic bag that Jax had pulled from her bag and placed in my lap was moving. As I stared at it, my eyes widened. "Jax. What is this? It's moving and it's totally freaking me out right now."

Jax picked it up and smiled. "Oh, that's the crab magnet I bought for Reign. I almost forgot about it." She unwrapped it and it reached its claws out and snapped them at Holly.

Holly clung to the door. "Eww. That's freaky Jax! It almost looks like a real crab."

"Right?" said Jax with a smile.

"Yeah, Jax. It's creepy. Shut it off." I reached over and took the crab from her hands. It tried to pinch me with its pinchers, but I held it so it couldn't get me. Then I flipped it over to shut it off, but couldn't find the off switch or a spot to remove the batteries. There was only a magnet back there. "Jax. How did you turn this thing on?"

"I didn't turn it on."

"Well, you had to. It wasn't snapping like that when I looked at it at that convenience store."

She frowned and shrugged. "Nope. I didn't do anything."

I lowered my brows. A lot of weird things seemed to be happening around Jax lately. "We still haven't had a chance to talk about what went down with Emily and with those bees in the RV. That was some weird stuff. Plus this crab? Something weird is going on, Jax."

"Yeah, I agree with Red. That's weird. What are you doing to make all of that happen?"

Jax shook her head. "Nothing! I swear." She sniffled a little. "I mean, I guess I've been sneezing a lot."

As the memories of Jax's sneezes flooded back, I couldn't help but nod. She'd sneezed on Emily, and she'd sneezed on the bees covering the Scotty Bee's to-go bag. "Did you sneeze on that crab in the convenience store?"

Jax shrugged. "Maybe."

Sweets sucked in her breath. "Oooh, Jaxie! I think you figured out your magic!"

Jax's eyes widened and she leaned forward to hug to the headrest in front of her. "What?! You think so?"

"It makes sense, Jax. You sneezed on the crab in the convenience store, and look. It's alive. You sneezed on Emily and she turned into a real unicorn," I said, shrugging.

Holly nodded. "And you sneezed on that to-go bag that had bees all over it. You brought the bees to life."

Alba shook her head. "Wow. That's so cool, Shorty. You can bring inanimate objects to life. I wish I could do that."

Jax was speechless as her eyes welled up with tears. She covered her mouth with her hand and shook her head gently, as if in awe of her own powers.

I gave her a nudge with my elbow. "Well? Say something, Jax."

She looked at me, a smile on her face. "I don't know what to say."

"Are you excited about your new powers?"

"I'm amazed," she admitted, her head slowly moving up and down. "I never thought I'd be able to do anything cooler than moving something just by pointing my finger, or cooler than seeing ghosts, or talking to animals, or reading someone's mind or predicting their future, or making someone love someone else. I never thought I'd be able to do anything like that. I think I'm still in shock that I was the one that brought Emily to life. And I brought this crab to life. And those bees. That's amazing!"

"Yeah, it is," agreed Alba. "It's pretty clear. You're *officially* a witch now, Jax. You've got real powers."

"I do have real powers!" Jax clasped her hands together and squealed. "This is so exciting! I can't wait to tell my ..." She stopped talking then and looked out her window.

I patted her leg. "It's okay, Jax. Your mom will be happy for you. She gave up her powers for you. You should call her and share your good news."

Jax wiped away a tear and nodded. "Yeah, I will when we get back to Aspen Falls," she whispered. "I just feel bad is all."

"Don't feel bad. If anyone deserves this, Jax, it's you," said Holly.

"Yeah, you do," said Sweets. That was when Sweets inhaled a deep breath. "Hey, girls. I didn't want to say anything before because after everything that happened, setting us back all that time, I didn't think anyone would want to. But now I feel like it's the right time."

"Right time for what?" I said. "What are you talking about, Sweets?"

"Just trust me," said Sweets. "I have an idea for the best tourist destination. It's the perfect way to cap off this trip and the school year and just... I don't know. Cement our friendship."

"Well, now you have me curious," said Holly. "Where do you want to stop?"

Sweets looked over at Alba. "Mind if we make one last stop before we leave town? I swear I won't ask to stop anywhere else the entire way to your house. Well, except at truck stops to use the restroom and get gas. But other than that, we'll make it a straight shot to New Jersey."

Alba crooked a brow at Sweets. "We'll still be home by this afternoon?"

"Oh, for sure," said Sweets, nodding.

Alba shrugged. "Alright. *One* roadside attraction. Let's do it."

Sweets smiled. "Yay! Oh, you girls are gonna love this."

CHAPTER 33

Whe pulled up to the front of a pretty basic, nondescript tan stuccoed building with a big green roof. The doors were painted brightly, but no one really paid attention to the sign above the door because as we all sat in the car, we were wondering if Sweets had somehow gotten us lost again. But when she turned off the ignition and swiveled around in her seat, announcing, "Here we are!" we all furrowed our brows.

"Here we are? Sweets, where are we?" asked Holly, looking to both sides of the road.

Everyone ducked their heads to look out the window in all directions.

Sweets pointed at the big building beside our car. "The Baltimore Tattoo Museum."

"We drove out of our way to go to a tattoo museum?" asked Alba with a quirked eyebrow. "I thought you were gonna take us to see the biggest goldfish on record or something. Why are we at a tattoo museum?"

"Well, for starters, because it's a roadside attraction, but it's more than that." Sweets let out a sigh. "It's actually a tattoo shop too. I was thinking that maybe we could all get a small tattoo. Like a friendship thing."

"Sweets!" I said, marveling at the fact that I couldn't believe *Sweets* would actually want to get a tattoo. "That's such a cool idea!"

"You gotta be kiddin' me, Red. You actually think this is a good idea?"

"I think it's an awesome idea." I'd always wanted to get a tattoo, but I'd never gotten around to actually *doing* it.

"We're almost out of cash. How are we supposed to pay for five tattoos?" said Alba.

"Oh, well, I thought it would be my gift to you girls. If we get it small enough, I don't think it'll cost that much. But I want to pay for it." Sweets smiled. "Now hear me out. I thought of it when Jax finally got her powers on graduation, but we've been so busy I haven't had time to bring it up. But now that we know that Jax *actually* has powers and can use them—well, kind of use them—I thought it would be cool to get matching witch tattoos. Something that represented the craft. Something that represented friendship. And since we're doing it on our road trip, I thought it would be cool if we got something that kind of symbolized that too. So, I designed a little something. We don't have to use it if you don't like it, but you can tell me what you think."

She opened up the glove compartment of her car and pulled out a slip of paper. On it, she'd designed a sort of compass with a witch's knot symbol in the center.

She pointed at it. "The compass represents our journey together and how, no matter where we are on this earth, we'll always know which way home is and that's wherever we are together. The witch's knot is a form of protection, and it's symbolic of not only our powers as witches, but also our friendship being bound together. Of course, the four points of the compass represent the four cardinal directions, but they also represent fire, air, earth, and water." She gave a little shrug. "We don't have to do it if you girls don't want to. I just thought it would be a powerful statement about our friendship."

Jax was the first to blurt out, "I'm in!"

I nodded. "Yeah, for sure. I've been wanting to get a tattoo forever. I just never knew what I should get. But I always thought whatever it was should be meaningful. This is about as meaningful as I could ever think of myself."

Alba glanced back at Holly. "What do you think, Cosmo? You're the one who thinks her body is a temple. You really wanna mar your temple with a tat?"

"My mother would *kill* me," said Holly, her blue eyes widening. "But, you know what? I'm in. You girls have been the best friends I've ever had in my life. Sure, I've had friends before, but they aren't the kind you make and keep forever. You girls are. So, I want to be a part of this. My mom will get over it eventually." She giggled. "Just like Dad will have to get over me using his credit card."

We all looked at Alba. "Well, Alba? It's your call," I said. "What do you think?"

Alba took the piece of paper from Sweets. "This *is* pretty cool."

Sweets' cheeks flushed red. "Thanks."

She looked up smiling. "And I can't let you guys do this without me. I'm in."

"Awesome!" cheered Jax.

Two hours later, we walked back out onto the sidewalk with matching tattoos adorning the insides of our wrists.

"I love it," said Jax, unable to stop staring at it.

"I do too," I agreed. "I can see how tattoos might be addictive. I'm totally getting another one someday."

"Tony's gonna flip when he sees it," said Alba, smiling broadly. "But I think he'll like it."

"What do you think, Holly?" asked Sweets.

"I think it's cute. It'll look really cute if I wear bracelets on this wrist with it. What do you think, Sweets?"

"Oh, I love it. But what I mostly love is that we all got the same one, and we did it together."

"Yeah, ditto," I said, nodding. "Thank you, Sweets."

"Yeah, thanks, Sweets," added the rest of the girls.

When the chatter died down, I had one last suggestion to make. "Hey, girls, before we leave, how about we do a quick friendship spell on our tattoos? Sweets said the witch's knot represented our friendship being bound. We could seal the deal with a quick spell. What do you think?"

Jax held out her hands and took a step backwards on the sidewalk. "Let's do it."

Sweets, grinning from ear to ear, took hold of Jax's hands and then held out her own hand.

One by one, we all joined the circle.

"You wanna start it out, Red?"

"Sure." I closed my eyes and tilted my chin up so I faced the sky. I felt my body absorbing the energy around us as I knew the rest of the girls were doing too.

"Friendship eternal, steadfast and true,
Oh, Great Spirits we call upon you.

We call to the Spirits of the North and of Earth

We witches are sisters more now than if joined by birth.
Please bless these symbols on our arms,
Strengthen our bond, and protect us from harm.

We call to the Spirits of the South and of Fire
Blessing our coven is what we desire.
Like a flame that burns and blazes free,
Our eternal connection we submit to thee.

We call to the Spirits of the East and of Air,
Our kindred spirit is the bond that we share.
Harness the power of a raging gale,
To strengthen our sisterhood, may it never fail.

We call to the Spirits of the West and of Water,
Born of you, we are pure hearted daughters.
Like a wild river rushing fast,
Make us five powerful witches at last.

Grant us this bond, and through our solemn connection,
We ask for your blessings, gifts, and protection."

Once I'd spoken the words, air began to whip up around our shoulders, making our hair fly and our clothing move.

The group of us chanted together the next time, making the leaves on nearby trees rustle and dust fly up into the sky. We chanted louder and louder as the energy filled our bodies. Performing the chant, I felt more powerful than I'd ever felt before. Like somehow we'd completed our circle. I felt stronger, like suddenly, our witches' coven had truly been blessed by the spirits.

We recited the chant one last time and then separated

our hands. The wind died down and settled our hair back onto our shoulders, and our clothes stopped moving.

"Wow," said Jax breathlessly, looking down at her hands. "That was more powerful than I thought it would be."

Alba nodded. "I have a feeling that *we* are more powerful than we realize."

Holly leaned her head on Sweets' shoulder.

Jax took my hand again and squeezed it.

I nodded. "I think *together* we're more powerful than we realize. Which is exactly why we have to keep our friendship strong. No more fighting."

Sweets smiled at me. "I agree with Mercy. No more fighting. Right, Alba?"

Alba nodded. "Yeah. I know. Having our own place next year will make a big difference, don't you think Cos —Holly?"

Holly smiled at her. "Yeah, for sure. A summer apart is going to make a difference too. I'm really going to miss you girls."

Jax brought us all in for a group hug. "I'm going to miss you all too."

When the hug was over, I couldn't help but smile. I loved these girls. I'd never thought I would say that about anyone outside of my family. But now they *were* my family. I put my newly tattooed wrist in front of me. "Witch Squad on three?"

Jax giggled and put her wrist in too. Then Sweets and Holly followed. Alba was last. She kind of rolled her eyes when she did it, but she did it, putting her wrist next to mine.

"One, two, three…"

"Witch Squad!"

EPILOGUE

That weekend, we dropped Alba off in plenty of time for her brother's wedding. We even got invited to stay. Which we did. It was nice seeing Alba with Tony. They made a cute couple. We also got to hang out with her parents and her brothers, and we quickly came to the realization that, as crazy as it sounded, Alba was the friendly one in the family.

Our goodbye to her, late Monday night after the wedding, was succinct. She didn't want to cry, so she slammed the door in our faces after we left. But she hollered through the door at us, "I'll miss you nerds." Then I was pretty sure I heard her choke up, but she'd never admit it if she did.

The ride home was bittersweet. It was nice finishing up the road trip with the girls, singing and laughing, playing dumb car ride games, and stopping at weird roadside attractions so we could get a few selfies in. I mean, without a few selfies amongst girlfriends, did a road trip even happen?

Ultimately, though, a weird feeling of dread hung in the

air. Mostly because we all knew that when we got Holly back to Aspen Falls, she'd have to pack her stuff for her flight to California, and we'd have to say goodbye to her for the rest of the summer too.

Sweets, Jax, and I had a big responsibility to the rest of the girls. We had to find us a place to live for the fall. But I wasn't worried. We had all summer to do it. Something would pop up.

In the meantime, Jax and I promised Mom and Reign we'd work at the B&B until school started in the fall. I didn't mind. I needed something to pass the time until the whole crew was united once again. I was thankful I had my new tattoo. I looked at it often. It reminded me not only of the girls, but of the amazing adventure we'd had together on our first summer break.

It had been a hectic year at the Paranormal Institute for Witches. At one point in my life, I'd wanted to just be a normal girl, so I could fit in with the rest of the kids I knew. But now that I'd had an opportunity to get to know the rest of the crazy band of misfits that I called friends, I realized I wouldn't trade being a witch for being a normal girl, and I wouldn't trade my friends for anyone else in the world. I was finally proud to be different.

And as I thought about my life and who I wanted to be and what I wanted to do as I got older, I found myself having one simple recurring thought. *I couldn't wait for what was to come.*

A NOTE FROM M.Z.

WOW! Can you believe the first year has come to a close? It's been quite the adventure for five misfits that somehow now *fit*. I've enjoyed every minute writing about this cast of characters! And the girls have already started making plans for year two! So I hope you're signed up for my newsletter, because then you'll be the first to know when the next book in Season 2 comes out! And let me tell you... there are some *big things* ahead of them that you're not going to want to miss!

And, as always, if you enjoyed the book and/or the series, please consider leaving a short review. It doesn't have to be much, just a few words really. It's the best way for others to learn about my books and keep me writing the stories you love. :) When I know you want more, it makes me want to write more!!

Thanks again for reading. You truly are the best readers a writer could ever want!

All the best,

M.Z.

ALSO BY M.Z. ANDREWS

Other Books Set in Aspen Falls in Reading Order

Witch Squad Book #1 - The Witch Squad - Season 1

Witch Squad Book #2 - Son of a Witch

Witch Squad Book #3 - Witch Degrees of Separation

Witch Squad Book #4 - Witch Pie

Witch Squad Book #5 - A Very Mercy Christmas

Witch Squad Book #6 - Where Witches Lie

Witch Squad Book #7 - Witch School Dropout

The Coffee Coven #1 - That Old Witch!

The Coffee Coven #2 - Hazel Raises the Stakes

Witch Squad Book #7.5 - Witch, Please!

The Coffee Coven #3 - That Crazy Witch!

Witch Squad Book #8 - The Witch Within

Witch Squad Book #9 - Road Trippin' with my Witches

The Coffee Coven #4 - That Broke Witch!

Witch Squad Book #10 - Welcome Back Witches - Season 2

The Mystic Snow Globe Mystery Series

Deal or Snow Deal: A Prequel

Snow Cold Case: Book 1

Snow Way Out: Book 2

The Witch Island Series

Behind the Black Veil: Book 1

Made in the USA
San Bernardino, CA
30 July 2020